THE MATTER OF THE DEMATERIALIZING ARMORED CAR

UNITED STATES DEPARTMENT OF TREASURY CAPER

STEVE LEVI

PUBLICATION CONSULTANTS

We Believe In The Power Of Authors

PO Box 221974 Anchorage, Alaska 99522-1974
books@publicationconsultants.com—www.publicationconsultants.com

ISBN 978-1-59433-751-2
eBook ISBN: 978-1-59433-752-9
Library of Congress Catalog Card Number: 2018935163

Manufactured in the United States of America.

There is never a moment when you
should not be Triple-C:
Calm, Cool and Collected.

. . . .Heinz Noonan

MONDAY

Chapter 1

Captain Heinz Noonan, the "Bearded Holmes" of the Sandersonville, North Carolina, Police Department, was hard at work on an unresponsive bagel when the first call of Monday morning came in. Setting the rock-hard-yet-hot circle of baked dough on a pile of interoffice memos, he reached for the phone.

Unfortunately for him, it was not the desk phone ringing.

The ringing came from the spawn of the devil, the "Great Disrupter" of all things holy and rational: his cell phone. Noonan was no enemy of progress, just certain aspects of progress—most specifically and uniquely, the cell phone. It was the disturber of the natural order of things. It brought communication with individuals with whom he had nothing in common but air, water, and the love of chocolate. You could converse with friends and family at your leisure and pleasure, but the cell phone brought a world of disreputable fellows and their collaterals to your door—or, rather, to your ear. Even more deleterious, you were joined at the hip with the evil incarnate.

Worst of all were the malevolent, malicious, and villainous individuals who viewed—and used—the electronic goblin as a means of supervisory control. In Noonan's life, these individuals were limited to one: Sandersonville Commissioner of Homeland Security Edward Paul Lizzard III, Napoleonic of stature but with the brainpower of a gnat. Captain of Detectives, Heinz Noonan, was the commissioner's favorite "cell phone buddy"—as the commissioner said on too many occasions—because Noonan "got things done." In a world of *manyana* people who worked on "river time," Noonan was stand-alone because he was a "finisher." When the commissioner "asked" something to be done, Noonan complied. Noonan complied quickly because he wanted as little as possible to do with the Commissioner of Homeland security, homeland security, or homeland in general. Noonan was so dedicated to the discovery and prosecution of murderers, burglars, and other disreputable folk in the Sandersonville environs that he had little time for chasing illusory, suspected, phantomlike, embedded Isis sharia-peddling operatives undercover, lurking and planning some dastardly deed in Sandersonville, North Carolina, a beach community where there were more T-shirt shops than there were mosques between Key West, Florida and Madawaska, Maine.

But Commissioner of Homeland Security Edward Paul Lizzard was—and it was a very sizable and important *was*—Noonan's immediate supervisor, so Noonan, unfortunately, had to take the call.

"Noonan here."

"Ah, Captain," the voice on the other end of the line began both smoothly and politically correct. "It's so good for you to be in your office."

"Really?" Noonan snapped within one iota of edge less than insubordination. "I decided to take the morning off from looking for burglars, rapists, and murders just to be here to take your call."

"You are such a card, Noonan." This comment was followed by a socially and politically correct chuckle.

Noonan tried to speed the call along. "I try to satisfy. Was there a reason for your call (pause because, to overuse a metaphor, Noonan could only poke the tiger in its cage), Commissioner?"

"Yes, as a matter of fact. A rather interesting matter came to my attention this morning."

"I see." The short sentence was as noncommittal as Noonan could be. "And . . ." He let the sentence end there.

"It's an interesting case."

"And . . ."

"Exactly your cup of tea."

"And . . ."

"You are free for a few hours, yes? This should not take long."

"And . . ."

"Excellent. I'll have John Swensen of the Swensen Armored Car Company give you a call. Seems he's lost one of his armoreds."

"Lost? As in stolen?"

"Nothing so *dramatic*, Captain. It's just vanished. En route to a pickup."

"En route? So it was empty. Had no money inside?"

"Probably not. This is not a robbery. It's one of those cases you are so good at solving. You know, a 'what's happening here?'"

"Well, sir . . ."

"Commissioner."

"Well, Commissioner, this does not sound like a police matter. I mean, with no money stolen, there is no crime; just a missing vehicle. Now if the armored car had been stolen, it would be another matter. As it is, we, your department, is up to its elbows in real crimes."

"This won't take long, Noonan. Not for a man of your caliber. I'm sure you can wrap this up rather quickly. Maybe by this afternoon. Do a good job so we can look good in the newspapers."

We, thought Noonan with a grimace. *You mean you.* But before he could utter another word, the phone went dead.

Chapter 2

Lenny Rusnak was a drinker, not a druggy. This was not meant to imply he was an alcoholic, a habitual drunk or anything close to it. In his younger days, yes, he had been a drunk; but a Friday-Saturday-night drunk. He didn't drink during the week but on those weekends! Then he just stopped. Saw too many of his friends get DUIs. In those days he could not afford even one DUI. Actually, he could not afford one even now.

But he was as close to a druggy now as he had ever been. *Unfortunately*, his friends said, *fortunately*, his VA doctor told him, and *perforce* he had to say, the drugs were legal. Three tours in Iraq and one in Afghanistan left him with a habit: Sertraline, Paroxetine, Fluoxetine, and Venlafaxine. In the old days, a cocktail was the starting gun of an evening of adventure. These days it was a brutal reminder of what he wanted to forget.

Colorado Springs was a *long* way in miles from Mosul, Sadr City, and Kandahar—during the day. But at night, they were as close as his pillow.

Over the years, he'd been getting better. He had hung up his uniform, got married, and was slip-sliding into the American middle class. After all, he was a successful entrepreneur. He had sales outlets in Fort Collins, Boulder, and Denver in addition to the two here in Colorado Springs. All the sales were doing a land-office business, and he was planning yet another two, one in Grand Junction and another in Pueblo. He had dreams of opening other operations out of Colorado, of going national. Big-time. The demand was there, but the supply was not.

That being said, there were seven problems to expanding across the Colorado border: New Mexico, Utah, Wyoming, Nebraska, Kansas, Oklahoma, and Arizona.

Recreational marijuana was not legal in those states. Yet. Legalization was coming fast, but it wasn't here yet. But until it was nationwide, he had one very large problem to solve.

Chapter 3

Noonan was still battling the rock-hard bagel an hour later when the next call came in. Setting the recalcitrant circle of baked dough on his desk blotter, he answered the phone.

The office phone this time.

"Is this Chief of Detectives Heinz Noonan?"

"Hope so. I'd hate to think I'm answering someone else's phone."

"Yeah, that could be a problem. Hey, I hate to bother you this early on a Monday morning, but I've got a problem that might be a crime. But then, again, it might not."

Noonan looked at the bagel. "Well, I've got a circle of rock-hard dough that might be a bagel but then, again, it might not. But let's hear your problem first."

"Actually, I can probably solve your problem faster than you can solve mine. If it's a hard bagel, put it in a microwave with a cup of water. Give it a thirty-second blast, and the water will make the bagel softer."

"Not a bad suggestion. I'll give it a try. Now, how about your problem?"

"Hopefully this is a wasted phone call. My name is John Swensen, and I'm the president and owner of the Swensen Armored Car Company here in Sandersonville. Your commissioner, Lizzard, suggested I give you a call. It seems one of our vehicles has gone missing."

"Missing?"

"Right. It went into a tunnel and never came out."

"There's only one tunnel in this area, the Pamlico Tunnel. Between Sandersonville and Pamlico City. Is that the one you mean?"

"Yes."

"It's not very long."

"Correct. But long enough for an armored truck to disappear."

"The armored truck went in and never came out?"

"I know how crazy it sounds, Captain, but it's the truth. It went in and never came out."

"Heinz."

"Sorry?"

"Heinz. When I'm investigating a crime, I'm Captain Noonan. But usually just captain. So far there is no crime here."

"Fine with me, Heinz. What we have is a missing armored truck. So far. No money stolen. Just a missing armored."

"What about the armored drivers?"

"Disappeared as well. We don't know where they are. What makes it more perplexing is that we had four men, guards, on motorcycles watching the vehicle—two in front and two in back."

"And they didn't see anything?" Noonan was incredulous.

"Zip."

"You had four men on motorcycles, two in front of the armored and two behind it, and the truck just poofed away? They didn't see anything? The armored was just gone?"

"It's a little more complicated than that."

"I hope so. I'm not into black magic."

"The armored disappeared into a tunnel. The guards were following procedure. There were two men on motorcycles at the entrance to the tunnel and two at the exit. The construction crew was only letting a few vehicles through at a time. In convoys. Two motorcycles went through first and secured the exit to the tunnel. That left other two behind. Then the armored car went through. Once the armored vehicle was out the other side, the two men at the entrance to the tunnel would go through. This is all standard for cases like this."

"Why?"

"A matter of insurance more than anything else. If there were to be an attempt on the armored truck in a tunnel, we don't want any civilians getting hurt. If there were a firefight in the tunnel, such things are bound to happen. Statistically. So, we don't escort the armored vehicles into tunnels. We send some guards to the far side to cover the exit. The armored vehicle enters the tunnel, and the guards in back cover the back door. It's what we call the 'back door.'"

"I see," said Noonan. "So your people followed procedure."

"To the letter."

"And then?"

"Nothing. The two forward guards went through the tunnel and set up on the far side. The armored went into the tunnel with a convoy, while the other two guards stayed at the entrance. When the convoy got to the other side of the tunnel, the armored car was gone."

"What did the escort on the other side of the tunnel say?"

"There was a conversation among the guards, and then one of the guards from the exit side of the tunnel came back. He was looking to see if the armored had stalled in the tunnel or was with another convoy."

"But it wasn't there."

"Correct. The tunnel was empty."

"Then things got very crazy very fast, right?"

"You got that right," Swensen said. "Very crazy, very fast." He paused for a moment. "All the guards agreed the armored car was gone. The men at the entrance watched the armored vehicle go into the tunnel, but the men on the other side did not see it come out."

Noonan shook his head as if to clear his thinking. "I don't want you to think I'm an idiot, but what I hear you saying is your guards saw an armored car go into a tunnel, and it never came out the other side. We're talking about the Pamlico Tunnel, aren't we? It's only about two or three thousand feet long."

"Right. The armored car went into the west end of the Pamlico Tunnel and didn't come out the east end."

Chapter 4

Curtis Jackson was a bankster—and he had no apologies for the characterization. He also had no qualms, hesitation, regrets, or remorse about his choice of occupation. Nor did he have any fear of eternal retribution. He wasn't doing the devil's work; he was doing the bank's work. His bank. As the majority shareholder, he *was* the bank. Banking was a crooked business; the law of supply and demand an academic delusion. Everyone in banking was cheating their customers, cutting quality corners, lying to their shareholders, fudging on their corporate tax forms, committing insider trading, colluding, hiding assets, and perpetrating every manner and shade of deception known and unknown to auditors, regulators, accountants, and examiners. The banksters could do it because they were *banksters*, and, as everyone knew, you can steal more with a pen than a gun—and Jackson was mighty with the pen.

Jackson had no shame because he was, after all, a bankster. Banksters, like defense lawyers, are immune to shame. Shame is not an occupational hazard in either of these industries. Jackson was privileged: institutionally, historically, legally, and personally. He was in an industry that was too big to fail, and banksters were too big to be jailed.

Jackson relished the fact he was knee-deep in a Shakespearean banking drama. The problem: he was not sure which drama was involved—*Much Ado About Nothing* or *Hamlet* or *Macbeth* or *Julius Caesar*. It was a modern drama to be sure, but whether it was a comedy or a tragedy had yet to revealed. All he knew—to be sure—was that the drama was quite complicated.

Legality was another matter altogether.

But then again, he was into banking, which was a Shakespearean world of its own. Every banker worth his or her salt was Iago, the

Janus of *Othello*. The industry was replete with Cassius and had more than a few Shylocks—of both *The Merchant of Venice* and the streets of American cities, large and small. It was an industry that had no laws, only limits. It was not as if there was a legal precipice, and one step over the lip doomed you to fall into oblivion. Or, fail into oblivion. Rather, what was *legal* in the banking community depended on three things happening.

In unison.

First, you had to make sure what you were doing was not perceived to be a Lone Ranger action. If every other bank was doing it, well, *they* could not get you all. The logic was, of course, it *must be legal* if everyone was doing it. After all, if the state and federal regulators did not *do* anything about what you were doing, it was legal. The regulators were the deciders. Banksters did not go to courts; they went to arbitration meetings. If ever a bankster should have gone to jail, it would have been in the Subprime Mortgage debacle of 2007 to 2009. Twenty-two trillion dollars was lost over a two-year period, and not a single bankster went to jail.

Jackson was well aware of the reason no banksters went to jail. It was a simple reality and could be summed up in three letters: SOP. What had been done was SOP, which is "Standard Operating Procedures." If what the banks had been doing had been illegal, someone would have been prosecuted long before the debacle. So, from a bankster's point of view, what the industry was doing was legal because no one had been prosecuted. Then why had there been a subprime mortgage debacle? Why, it was a black swan, a recently coined financial/economic term for an event causing a major effect that could only be understood with hindsight. In terms of the street—Main, not Wall—it was the epitome of "they never saw it coming." This, with hindsight, was a crock because the disaster was twenty-twenty in the eyes of some investors, and they made a killing selling the crisis short—and earned starring reference in the hit movie *Selling Short*.

But still, not a single bankster went to jail.

Second, it was illegal if what you were doing was less than an arm's length transaction. If there was no paper trail linking the decision-maker at the bank with the alleged-to-be violation of the law, said action was a down-the-administrative-chain error. Error is not felonious. Felony stupidity is not a crime. Both changed the critical aspects of a fiscal decision. You could move whatever money you wanted *as long as* there was a buffer between you and the initial transaction. A bankster could not let his bank pay off his own home loan and then write off the mortgage income loss as a bad debt for the bank. But a bankster across town could arrange for *his* bank to buy *your* mortgage while *your* bank bought *his* mortgage. Then, mysteriously, if both mortgages "went bad," there was nothing illegal going on. There was no paper trail connecting the two transactions. No paper trail, no crime. No harm, no foul even if you and the other banker ended up living in mortgage-free homes. As long as no bank lost money, all was well in both banks. So the feds ended up with the losses. Such was the business.

Third, and most important, the greatest danger was putting yourself on a financial investigator's radar. As long as a bankster stayed reasonably legal and did not get greedy, the bankster would be left alone. Annual audits were a laugh whether they were federal or state. Internal examinations were simply a rubberstamp for the annual report.

These three pitfalls being exposed, there was a rather delicious upside to the downside. If you were clever and dexterous, you could use the downside to your advantage. This was neither a hybrid of the old saw of "rules are made to be broken" nor a flaw in the regulatory fabric. It was simply a matter of being in the right place at the right time and *knowing* you were in the right place at the right time.

Then there was Caerus.

Caerus was the Greek god of opportunity, luck, and good fortune. For very good reason, he is a young man with wings on his back and heels. He and opportunity are fleeting. He is often depicted carrying a balance scale cementing the solid link between the god and the real world. What made Caerus prophetic was a single lengthy lock of hair extending from his forehead. He was the god of opportunity, luck, and good fortune *but*—and this was a rather substantial ***but***—you were only going to get one chance to snag good fortune as Caerus came zooming by. You were only going to get one chance—*uno, un,* *eins, ett, unus, odin, yksi*—to grab the single lock of hair. One and only one. So being in the right place at the right time was not enough. You had to seize the lock of hair before Caerus disappeared into the proverbial mist of time.

Caerus flew by Curtis Jackson, president of the First Sandersonville Bank of Trust, in the form of a disreputable individual: a brother-in-law. Curtis Jackson was no fool; he snatched the hair-lock.

The Jackson family, quite extended, were banksters, whose roots on the North Carolina coastline extended back to the first shipwreck survivors in the sixteen hundreds. As the Jackson family always said with prophetic humor, "If you were the first on the coast, all the land was free—and we were the first." The Lumbee Indians were first on the coast, of course, but over the centuries, the Jacksons married into the tribe, stole from the tribe, or simply waited for them to die off depending on which version of North Carolina history one cared to read.

The Jacksons had been coastal hillbillies, so to speak, until the 1920s when they discovered a new enterprise: banking. Rather, they stumbled into it. With cash oozing out of every pore of the body politic of the *nouveau riche* of the middle and northern east coast of Yankeedom, the Jackson family *ensemble* moved into the tourist trade. They opened small hotels where the proprietors were blind to the transgressions of their patrons. The family also had the local connections to make sure none of the *transgressions* of their renters resulted in paperwork, such as police reports or stories in local newspapers. Since the local newspapers and police departments were operated, owned, or opined by extended Jackson family members, what happened on the coastline of North Carolina and the Outer Banks stayed on the coastline of North Carolina and the Outer Banks.

From there the family moved into tourist gewgaws and novelty products. It did not take the family long to realize it had a cash problem. This was because of the unique character of an East Coast vacation. On the West Coast in the same time period, and to this day, a "vacation" is a single week. Two weeks, if you were lucky. But on the East Coast, one went on "holiday." Not "a holiday" but "holiday." It was singular and usually lasted six weeks. East Coasters "on holiday" came to the coastline of North Carolina and Outer Banks and stayed a month and a half. Every day of the month and a half, they ate, drank, lounged on the beach with beer (even though it was illegal in the early days of the tourism boom), and bought all manner of tourist products. It would not be until the next century before such commercial transactions would be primarily electronic. But for eighty years, the coastline of North Carolina and the Outer Banks ran on cash.

Thus did the Jackson family get into banking. The extended family took in extraordinary amounts of cash from the tourists but did not trust banks not owned by relatives. This was perfectly reasonable because, by the late 1920s, banks were going under faster than flocks of seagulls diving for baitfish. So the Jackson family opened its own banks, eventually six of them between Moorehead City and Corolla and inland as far as Vanceboro and Plymouth. Every one of the banks survived the Bank Holiday of 1933 and quickly became members of the FDIC.

Seventy years later the banks were still in business—not that banks ever go out of business. They are like casinos. If you cannot make a profit from a bank or a casino, you should get a job as a bureaucrat. But what made these banks so unusual was the excessive amounts of cash they had to keep on hand. The "holiday" trade was almost exclusively cash. This meant every beach business was depositing cash in the banks every night, from Memorial Day to Labor Day. But this cash could not be stored in the banks. First, because it was in small bills—mostly five dollars, ten dollars, and twenty dollars—which took up a lot of space. Second, while businesses did not need much cash Monday through Thursday, a lot of cash was needed during the balance of week. Then there was the Fourth of July, craft shows, traveling troubadours, and the state-operated hard-liquor stores. Banks needed the cash *on* hand—but not in *their* hand. So the banks began storing their excess cash with the Swensen Armored Car Company in Sandersonville.

This turned out to be a fortuitous turn of fortune. While it was a matter of convenience in the 1940s and 1950s, by the 1960s there had been a glacial change in the world of money: checks followed by credit cards—and then debit cards. In the 1940s and 1950s, everything had been cash-and-carry. By the 1960s, more and more people were paying with checks and credit cards. This reduced the amount of cash that tourist businesses had to have on hand, but it increased the risk of bad financial instruments. The coastal businesses were still demanding cash, but the larger purchases, such as housing rentals, could be done with a check or credit card because the tourist had to pay in advance. Then, as technology progressed, the financial instruments could be verified within seconds. Debit charges cleared instantly. There was no longer a need for American Express Traveler's Checks—"Don't leave home without them!"— and checks or, for that matter, cash. Then came the cell phone and the SquareUp. Yes, a certain amount of cash was still needed, but not as much as before.

But the collective banks still had millions in cash sitting in storage at the Swensen Armored Car Company vault.

This, however, was not a bad thing. This was because money—as in cash—was imaginary in the banking world. Cash does not exist. As an example, if you have $1,000 in your checking account, and you go to the bank to see your $1,000, the bank will laugh at you. Your $1,000 does not exist. Not even on paper. The only paper on which your $1,000 exists is your monthly statement. The rest of the time, your alleged $1,000 is an electronic pulse. But even though it is imaginary, you can still take a piece of plastic that is not linked with a wire to your bank and use that piece of plastic to buy things that do exist: apples, ground round, coffee, beer, and bananas. To buy those things that do exist, you do not even need pieces of paper identified as five-dollar, ten-dollar, fifty-dollar, or one-hundred-dollar bills.

But this is just the chicken-feed end of the banking system. Taking a step deeper into the reality of banking, suppose Business A delivers its weekend receipts, $10,000 in cash, to the bank on Monday morning. Instantaneously the $10,000 is in Business A's account. Business A now has $10,000 more than it had Friday at the close of banking hours. On Monday morning, the bank has $10,000 more money in its asset base. Because of the added $10,000 in its asset base, the bank can now legally lend out ten times the amount in loans. So the $10,000 in cash from Business A deposited at 9:00 a.m. is magically transformed to $100,000, which can be loaned out at one nanosecond after the 9:00 a.m. deposit from Business A.

But there was an added twist. Only $10,000 in cash came in, but $110,000 was created: the $10,000 in Business A's account and the $100,000 the bank can lend out. Suddenly the cash has no value. Business A is not going to ask for its $10,000 in cash back. And when the bank loaned out the $100,000, the loan is not going to be made in cash. It will be on a piece of paper linked to the banking system. No actual cash was transferred. Further, the $10,000 in cash coming in has no value. It was just paper sitting in the bank's vault.

Since the bank had more important use for the space in its vault than storage of one dollar, five dollar, ten dollar, twenty dollar, fifty dollar, and one hundred dollar bills, it made business sense to store the cash that would reasonably be needed quickly in a convenient location. On the coast of North Carolina, that convenient location was in Sandersonville, the heart of the tourism trade, in the vault of the Swensen Armored Car Company.

The only increasing value of the actual cash was the amount the Swensen Armored Car Company was charging for the monthly service to warehouse the cash. But the monthly fee saved the banks from warehousing stacks of boxes of five dollars, ten dollars, and twenty dollars in its own vault, a fireproof vault better suited for storing original loan documents. Besides, the actual *value* of the money had already been incorporated into the bank's legal assets. The bank was lending out ten times the amount of the cash taken in—in whatever form the cash was and wherever the cash happened to be.

None of this was a problem in the sense the Jackson collection of banks wanted to change the system. The growing collection of actual dollars was a paperwork nuisance, not a financial problem. But, as it turned out, it could be one shaft of a three-legged financial bonanza for the banks.

The second leg came courtesy of Caerus.

Two of Curtis Jackson's ne'er-do-well collaterals were working as drivers for the Swensen Armored Car Company. They were castoffs of a Jackson faction that was invested heavily in real estate because their land was on the Pamlico Sound side of the Outer Banks. Beachfront property on the Atlantic side of the Outer Banks was at a premium because it was, after all, beachfront. But because of hurricanes, global warming, and the blast of Atlantic storms, beachfront homes on the Atlantic side were often destroyed.

Which was why long-term residents of the Outer Banks built their homes on the Pamlico Sound side of the islands. The power of the hurricanes and Atlantic storms dissipated before reaching the other side of the string of islands. The tides were much less severe on the Sound side, and there were wetlands to break the power of the waves. Structures on the Sound side survived for generations, while those on the Atlantic shore had a significantly shorter shelf life.

By 2010, the beachfront on the Atlantic side of the Outer Banks was shoulder-to-shoulder-to-shoulder homes, which were hostages of every weather system between the Bahamas and New Jersey. The homes were built right to the edge of the National Park, and then there was no more beachfront room. Thereafter, courtesy of the law of supply and demand, weekly rental rents went up. As the national economy got better, more East Coasters went "on holiday" and the rates went up again.

When the rates got high enough, cruise lines began looking at the Outer Banks as a prime interim location for luxury hotels. Travelers could board a cruise liner in New York and leisurely proceed down the coast to Virginia Beach where they would be put on buses for Corolla, Duck, Sandersonville, Frisco, Hatteras, and Ocracoke for two or three days of beachcombing, deep-sea fishing, and historic tours of the shoreline where Blackbeard died, and ghosts of pirates still haunt the inlets and bights. Or, since many of the tourists were elderly, three days in the solitude of the Outer Banks.

But none of the cruise lines were willing to build on the Atlantic seacoast. The cost was too high and the risk too great. So, very quietly, the cruise lines began looking to invest in Pamlico Sound side property.

It may have been quiet from the point of view of the cruise lines, but the residents of the Outer Banks were not stupid. They knew low-level inquiries were going on. They could also read the tea leaves. So they went the cruise lines one better. Rather than have neighbor compete with neighbor for the lowest property sales price, they formed loose collectives and offered the cruise lines blocks of land for a reasonable price. After the infighting ceased, there were four competing collectives, all vying for the attention of the cruise lines, with none of them large enough for a luxury hotel complete with parking, dining facilities, docking area, and so on. And none of the collectives was willing to wheel and deal with the others. Further, no collective was going to take credit or a long-term lease. This was going to have to be a cash-and-carry sale with one hefty price tag.

So there the deal of a century sat with no collective large enough to profit. The only solution was for some entity other than a cruise line to buy all properties at the same time and then negotiate for a good price from the cruise industry.

But the clock was ticking.

If the cruise companies—in the singular or multiple—did not find a land deal in Sandersonville, well, then it was up or down the coast for another option.

Curtis Jackson knew an opportunity when he saw one.

He also knew the clock was ticking.

All he had to do was find one buyer who had $10 million in cash to buy out all the collectives at the same time. Then his bank could negotiate a substantially higher price for the land as well as keep an oar in the water for construction loans, long-term mortgages, ongoing maintenance accounts, and every other fiscal angle he could finagle.

As he was contemplating the sad state of affairs of a massive lucrative deal just beyond his financial fingertips, two ne'er-do-well Jacksons, Charlie and Harry, introduced him to the man of his fiscal dreams. Even better, this man wanted to buy out the collectives with cash.

Ten million dollars in a single transaction.

That man was Joseph Richiamo.

But there was a problem.

Chapter 5

In Noonan's eyes, the Swensen Armored Car Company was exactly what it appeared to be: a high-security garage. Noonan was expected, but it didn't stop the guard at the front gate from looking over his badge and making a photocopy of his ID card.

"We can't be too careful these days," the guard said as he handed Noonan back his badge case. "Today in particular."

"I know what you mean," replied Noonan as he slipped his ID case back into his pocket. He looked around the open yard of the Armored Car Company garage. The lot was empty.

"Is it usually this empty?" Noonan asked.

The guard looked up in surprise. "Sorry. Most people just get their IDs checked and wander inside. Is it usually this quiet? Yeah, sort of. We don't have a lot of milling around here. The armored cars are in the garage," the guard pointed to the large, warehouse-like structure, "and they get loaded there. Once the armored cars come out of the garage, they go right out the gate. We, the guards, do not check armored cars on their way in. That's done in the garage. By the vault. We just log them on the way out. Most of the time they are empty. We don't check the inside of the armoreds coming in either. We just make sure they get into the garage. When they get into the garage, that's when the security really kicks in."

"What do you mean by 'kicks in'?" Noonan asked.

"Well, when there's money, well, you know what I mean. We have to be a lot more careful who comes and goes."

"So you check IDs on the way in?"

"If we don't know you by face, yes, sir."

"How about cars driven by the guards? Do they get checked?"

"No one parks in here," the guard said, waving his arms around the yard. "They park on the other side of the fence over there." He pointed to a distant point on the cyclone fence topped with razor wire. "Then they walk in."

"Is everyone searched coming out?"

"Not *searched* as in patted down, no. But no one who works here comes in with a pack or a briefcase because he or she can't leave carrying anything. The only vehicles going out these gates without being searched are armored cars."

"And motorcycles."

"Yeah, and motorcycles. As long as you don't mean anything piled on a motorcycle. If something is on a motorcycle, like a large bag, we'd search it."

"How often has that happened?"

"Twice since I've been here."

"How long have you been working here?"

"Fifteen years."

"What was in the bags you searched?"

"Laundry. Both times. Uniforms going out to be washed."

"They, the bags, were escorted out?"

"No. The uniforms were in bags on the back of a motorcycle. There was no armored car, just the motorcycle. But rules are rules, so I checked the bags."

"When the armored cars leave here, do you know where they are going?"

"Sort of." The guard smiled. "The cops already asked me." He looked at Noonan suspiciously for a moment. "You're a cop, right? I've already been asked that."

Noonan smiled. "I'm not *that* kind of a cop. I look into unusual cases. Like this one. I'm not looking for money, just answers." The answer did not seem to satisfy the guard, so Noonan plowed forward in a different direction. "OK, let's try this another way. Generally speaking—and I don't know your business, so I'm just guessing— armored cars leave here for three purposes. First, to drive around and pick up deposits from businesses. Second, to deliver those deposits to banks. Third, to move things of value that aren't necessarily going from a business to a bank. Maybe like a valuable painting or a special delivery of gems."

"Wwweellll," the guard drew out the word, gaining confidence he was not on the hot seat, "what you said is generally true. Depending on the run, the armored car could make twenty or thirty pickups during the day but might also visit six banks and drop off deposits. Those trips are escorted. As far as the valuables, sure, we do handle some, but it's not a regular thing. I know when we've got a special delivery because the armored car goes out without an escort. That means whatever's inside is insured or the truck is empty."

Noonan smiled. "Well, let me be more specific. The armored truck that's missing. Did it have a regular route?"

"Same thing every Sunday, yeah. No secret there."

"So anyone could have known where and when the armored car was going to be at any one moment during the day?"

"Could have, but they'd have to be really good. The Jacksons . . . er . . . the drivers have been working here for as long as I have. They knew the routine and were sharp. Besides, they had an escort."

"But if the armored was empty, why the escort?"

"Sunday deliveries are always escorted. Businesses are open, but banks are not. It means the armoreds are full of cash and have to come back loaded. The big money, if you want to call it that, is on Monday. After the weekend. On Mondays the armoreds are stopping at banks along the way and making deposits. They are still picking up more money on Monday but arriving back here with a lot less than on a Sunday."

"So Sunday is the best day to rob an armored car?"

"Yeah, in terms of money, but it's a lot riskier for the bandits. There's less traffic on Sunday, which means more cops on the road. I'd guess you'd say it is a trade-off."

"How many times has a Swensen Armored Car Company car or truck been robbed?"

"Easy answer. None. Not since I've been working here. Our people are very careful."

"No trouble of any kind?"

"Some insurance quibbles but not with us. We get auditors through here pretty regularly, but they don't stay long. My guess, we're following the rules, so there's no reason to spend a lot of time going over our books."

"You know a lot about the business. For a guard, I mean."

The guard smiled. "We're like family here. We get moved around so everyone knows what's going on in the other parts of the business. That's the way John . . . er . . . Mr. Swensen likes it. It means he doesn't have to keep training new people. He just promotes from within. I've been a driver, an escort, worked in the records room, worked in the vault. Every part of the operation. We're the best paid in the business. That's why most of us have been here so long. And we all know the different jobs, so if someone is sick or on vacation, the replacement knows what the . . ." He stalled, searching for the right, clean word.

"Heck," Noonan helped him. "What the heck is going on?"

"You took the word right out of my mouth."

Both men laughed.

"I assume John Swensen is in the room labeled *office*?" Noonan pointed across the empty lot to the only set of windows beside a door on the warehouse wall.

"Better be," replied the guard. "The police have been in there for three hours, and I don't think they're alone."

Chapter 6

Lenny Rusnak was up to his eyeballs in what used to be called drug paraphernalia and was once illegal to sell. Today it was called inventory. But it was odd inventory, a reversal of seven hundred years of business advances. Double-entry bookkeeping, the concept of a fiscal balance between incoming and outgoing, debits and credits, had been in the historical record all the way back to the Republic of Genoa in 1340. This was a good two centuries before the root work of modern banking brought about by religious reformers, Luther and Calvin, sank into fertile fiscal soil of Christian Europe.

Technology, necessity, efficiency, greed, and suspicion had propelled the banks to become the mega giants they were. At the same time, Rusnak was in the one nation on earth at a singular time in world history where he could not bank his legally earned cash. While, at the same time, drug dealers, large and small, were using the banks with little federal or state oversight. The irony was that Rusnak was making legal money, and then he was stuck with the cash. *Stuck with cash,* an odd term to use in the United States of America in the twenty-first century, where using a bank was as close to a religion as football, drinking, or badmouthing your in-laws. He had cash, but there was nothing big he could do with it. He could buy groceries and beer but not a house, car, or certificate of deposit.

He was thus captured in a fiscal warp in the fabric of American civilization. Because marijuana was legal, he could sell it. In Colorado. But he could not put the money in a bank anywhere in America.

Further, because selling marijuana was legal—in Colorado—he needed a business license and had to pay taxes: business, income, property, and sales to the city and state. In Colorado. But at the same time in the same city and state, marijuana was listed as Schedule 1 narcotic by the federal government. Thus, it was—in the eyes and statutes of the federal government—an illegal substance. As such, no federally regulated institution could be associated with it. The biggest federally associated institution to be impacted were the banks. Even though banking is not mentioned in the United States Constitution, banks are regulated by the Securities and Exchange Commission and the Federal Deposit Insurance Corporation. What this meant on a nuts-and-bolts level was that no checks, debit cards, or credit cards could be used to buy marijuana or any of its products. It also meant any money earned from the legal sale of marijuana or any of its products was—again, in the eyes of the federal government— drug money and must be confiscated. So the marijuana industry was making money legally, paying legally owed taxes to the city and state governments, but was denied access to the use of banks.

Schizophrenically, even though marijuana was a Schedule 1 drug and technically illegal in the bureaucratic eyes of the federal government, this did not stop the same federal government bureaucracy from collecting income taxes from the same entrepreneurs it was excluding from the banking system.

Thus the rub: the industry was making money hand-over-fist but had a cash problem: too much of it. So what do you do with $1 million in cash—legitimately earned—if you cannot use a bank, cannot buy stock, cannot buy bonds, cannot buy real estate, and cannot invest in any of the panoply of financial opportunity open to anyone else in America, who has legal money to spend? Rusnak could not buy a house because it required going through a bank, and his money was oxymoronic: opposites combined to form a new reality. In figures of speech, it was easy to define: cruel kindness, living death, open secret, military music, and pretty awful. In the world of nuts and bolts, oxymorons were hard to find. Yet, in the cannabis business, it was standard. He was making money legally by state law, but it was illegal by federal law. So he was selling legal inventory but could not use any financial instrument available to even a derelict in an alley. The banks would not allow him to accept checks, credit cards, or debit carts. From there the list expanded. He could not transform his cash into certificates of deposit, checking accounts, savings accounts, government bonds, stocks, or even cashier's checks. Car dealerships would not take cash for a new car, and banks would not accept $250,000 in cash for a home. The United States Post Office would take small amounts of cash for postal orders, but his businesses were pulling in close to $250,000 a month. His profit was a modest 6.75 percent after taxes, but it was still cash. So he had no IRA, no 401K. There he sat, $200,000 a year income in cash, living in a $150,000 home that his wife was buying on paper because she had a *real job*.

He, a millionaire, was up to his ears in cash he could not invest.

Then, one day, along came Joseph Richiamo.

Chapter 7

Noonan circumnavigated the oil spots on the garage floor and made it into the Swensen Armored Car office just as John Swensen was giving two state troopers a rundown on what had happened.

"Like I said, officers," Swensen nodded at Noonan as the captain came into the office, "the cell-phone message I received was pretty strange."

Swensen took a moment to let Noonan introduce himself around. Then Noonan said, "I appear to be a bit late. I assume we are talking about messages from the stolen armored car." There was a chorus of yeahs. There were three other people in the room, two from the troopers and one was from an insurance company. Proof the third man was an insurance agent came when the man, a cadaverous scarecrow, gave Noonan a card, which Noonan glanced at and then pocketed.

"*Missing* armored car," Swensen corrected Noonan. "We don't know it's been stolen. Stolen is a legal term that implies we have lost a shipment. Which we haven't."

"Let's leave the hair-splitting to the lawyers." Noonan nodded to the others. "What did you mean by *strange?*"

Swensen looked at the two troopers hanging on his every word. One of them pulled out a pad, and she started to write what he said.

"Well," Swensen continued, "the first message, on the radio, said they, the drivers, were detouring to avoid an overturned vehicle. The second a short time later said they were picking their way around something. It was unclear what the something was. I assume they were talking about something in the tunnel. The next call came in on my cell phone, and the drivers said they were being foamed."

"Foamed?"

"Yes. It sounded like 'foamed.'"

"That was the last message?" Noonan asked.

"Right. Then the communications channel went ghost."

The trooper with the notepad shook her head. "Did you get the impression they actually saw an overturned vehicle? There were two drivers, right?"

"Right. Two. Did they actually see a vehicle? I think so. I'd have to listen to the tape again, but I think so."

"Foamed. Hmph." Noonan drummed his fingers on a desk. "Foamed," he repeated. "What was in the vehicle?"

"No money, if that's what you are asking. It was on a pickup route, not a collect-and-deposit run. The armored car was scheduled to go from business to business and pick up cash and credit card receipts from weekend sales. Then it would bring the cash and receipts here." He indicated the building with a wave of his hand toward one of the walls of the office. "We store the cash and receipts until Monday, then make deliveries to the bank."

"So the armored car was empty in terms of cash?"

"Correct."

"Is security any different for an empty armored car than a full one?"

"We're playing a vocabulary game here, Captain."

"Heinz."

"Sorry, Heinz. The armored car leaving the garage was empty. It was being guarded because it was going to be picking up money from seventeen or eighteen businesses. By the time it had picked up those deliveries, it would be 'full of money,' to use a generic term."

"How much money would it have been picking up?" the trooper with the pen and pad asked.

"I don't know. Some of the deliveries were for banks, so we picked them up in bank bags with locks and were to deliver them to the respective banks on Monday, today. I . . . we don't know how much money was in those deliveries. The other fifteen were businesses of various sizes. Figuring an average of twelve thousand dollars per business, we're talking about two hundred thousand dollars."

"In cash?"

"Not much of it. Not a lot of cash these days. Lots of paper—checks and credit and debit card readouts."

"So the security was the same as for any other delivery."

"Correct again."

Noonan looked at the other three and then said at Swensen. "Well, I'm sure the troopers are going to ask you about the possibility of this being an inside job."

"I anticipated that." Swensen pointed to a pile of folders on his desk. "I pulled the personnel files of the four motorcycle security men and the two drivers." Swensen scooped them up and handed them to Noonan. "There's a breakroom down the hall." He pointed to the left of his office door. "I'll see you are brought coffee. There should be all kinds of pens and paper in the office. The senior security man is George Steigle. He's cooling his heels in the hallway. Do you want to see him right away?"

"Absolutely," Noonan said.

Swensen stood up and looked at the three others in the room. "Why don't the three of you take a break? I have to make introductions with George, the senior security guard. I want to make sure he knows to answer all of Captain . . ."

"Heinz."

"Right. Heinz." Then, looking at the other three at the table, he said, "I want to make sure Steigle knows to answer all of Heinz's questions. After Heinz finishes with him, you can look over the details. Right now, you three are interested in any money that might have been stolen, not the armored that," Swensen raised his left hand and pointed an index finger at the three, "is *missing*, not stolen. There is no money missing, so this is an odd occurrence, but as yet there is no crime, and Harry," Swensen looked directly at one of the three, "there is no insurance claim pending because nothing is stolen. Got it?"

One of the three, the living skeleton who had handed Noonan his card, sort of nodded.

"I'll be right back," Swensen said and led Noonan out of the room.

The two went down a short hallway and entered what was clearly a breakroom. There were candy bar and soda dispensing machines all along one side of the room and a wall-to-wall bank of lockers across the room. The third wall was a side-by-side sink and stove combination. In the center of the room was a Formica table with piles of newspapers and magazines.

When Steigle came into the room, President Swensen motioned the security motorcycle man into an empty chair next to Noonan

"George," Swensen told the man. "This is Captain Heinz Noonan of the Sandersonville Police Department. I have asked for him to investigate the missing armored car. You are tell him everything you know about what happened. Hold nothing back. I am telling you this because there is every reason to believe the disappearance is a prank, not a robbery."

Steigle gave a you're-the-boss nod and extended his hand to Noonan for a shake. Noonan smiled and shook the extended hand.

As Swensen stood at the back of the breakroom, Steigle sat down opposite Noonan as Noonan cleared a portion of the table from the magazines. Then Noonan pulled out his notepad. Steigle was quiet. Noonan asked the guard if he wanted a cup of coffee. Steigle refused the offer.

"Nothing personal," Noonan began, "but you are a bit old for a security guard."

"Nothing personal about it," Steigle said in a soft voice, which surprised Noonan. "I'm not doing it for the money." He glanced over his shoulder at Swensen. Swensen gave his head a quick nod and rose from his chair by the door.

"I've got to get back to the troopers," Swensen said as he left the room.

Steigle hardly fit the image of a security guard. He was tall enough for a guard—a few inches over six feet and clearly worked out in a gym regularly—but there the stereotype ended. He was so lean his uniform was an odd fit over his sculpted body. He wore an Academy ring on his right hand and no wedding ring on his left. His nails were manicured and his hair perfectly coiffured. He had a pair of aviation sunglasses on his forehead, and a Fitbit protruded from beneath his right sleeve when he propped his elbows on the breakroom table.

Steigle waited until Swensen had left and the door closed. "Like I said," he continued, now looking directly at Noonan, "I'm not a security guard for the money. I'm retired and bored. So I took the job."

"What did you do before you rode for the Swensen Armored Car Company?"

"Lawyer. An incredibly boring job that paid too well to totally quit. Still does. In the old days, it was primarily corporate. Contracts, patents, labor disputes, more contracts and more contracts after that. Now I do wills, trusteeships, living wills, divorce settlements, and a lot of pro bono for people who cannot afford a lawyer. It's not a lot of fun, but it still pays, and I've got quite a few bills."

"Not a thrilling job, eh?"

"Not an iota of charm. Took up riding as a hobby. Then it became my mental escape. After I retired from the corporate world, I figured I'd try a job that required a bike."

"Motorcycle?"

"Right. We call it a bike."

Noonan smiled. "Your bike has a lot more power than the bike I learned to ride when I was a kid."

Steigle sort of smiled. "Yup."

"How long have you worked for Swensen?"

"Five or six years," Steigle replied. "Took it as a lark and took to liking it. Good people here. Like family. Sure, sorry this happened."

"Well, since you brought it up," Noonan picked up a pen from beside the notepad on the table, "what exactly did happen?"

"Unfortunately, I can't tell you about anything that was out of order. Everything was routine. Even for a Sunday."

"Was a Sunday delivery unusual?"

"As a security guard, no. I and the others arrive when we are told to arrive. Monday or Sunday, be it noon or at 8:00 a.m. We don't make the schedule; we just follow it. In the five years I've worked here, I have to say no time is *unusual* the way you mean it. I think the schedule is made to fool robbers, if you know what I mean— scramble the schedule."

"So it was just a normal day for you?"

"Normal job. I don't work days like in a regular job. I show up when I'm needed and get paid by the hour."

"How many hours do you work in a month?"

"Not as many as I would like, but as long as I'm no more than half-time, I can keep getting my Social Security check."

"Gotta keep busy. Good for you. Now, tell me what happened when you got to work on Sunday."

"Well, there were four of us. I was senior, so I took the lead. I did the check-in. It was all routine. I got to garage, and I was given our manifest. The armored car was ready to go when I got here. I checked the front license plate against the manifest and left. Then—"

"No. Just a minute. There were four of you around the armored car?"

"No. Just me. I did the checking. In the garage. That's the way it's done. The lead goes into the garage, does the check-in. The other three are on their bikes in the yard. Then I came out and got on my bike. When I did, it was the signal to start the escort."

"OK. Now, how many people were in the armored?"

"Two. Charlie and Harry. I know 'em."

"How well?"

"Very well. More than by sight. We're a tight group here at Swensen. We get moved around a lot, so we've all worked with one another."

"Do Charlie and Harry ever ride motorcycles?"

"No. I guess I misspoke. Here at Swensen we all get a taste of everyone else's job. That's the way John . . . er . . . Mr. Swensen keeps us one big happy family. We all know the routine because we've worked all the jobs. But there aren't many of us on bikes. Charlie and I usually ride bikes."

"Charlie?"

"Schanche. He was on the back with me yesterday. He's been on bikes as long as I've known him here. I don't think he's done any other job at Swensen. He's . . . how should I say it . . . a burned-out vet. He's happy to be riding bikes. The two drivers—the Jacksons—Charlie and Harry, are not bike people. They don't want to be bike people and would be a danger on a bike. So, no, they have not had a turn at riding security. But, yes, I know them by sight. They were in the armored."

"Did you check to see if there was anyone inside the back?"

"No. I just checked the front license plate against the manifest. It matched. I signed off the security sheet and dropped it off on the desk inside the garage as we were leaving."

"Did you walk around the armored at all? I mean, did you check to see if the license on the back matched the license on the front of the armored?"

"No. Like I said, the license plate on the front bumper matched the manifest, so I waved the armored out of the garage."

"Who was there when you left? I mean in the garage and at the front gate?"

"Well, we, all of us, checked in with the guard at the front gate. He knows us, so he just waved us in. We got the bikes out of the mechanical shop and parked them in the lot. Then I went into the Security Room and was given the manifest."

"Where were our other three guards?"

"In the yard on their motorcycles."

"But not in the garage?"

"Correct. I went into the garage alone."

"Is that standard? I mean, is that the way it's usually done?"

"Yeah. The garage is not large, so getting four bikes inside with the armored cars makes a tight squeeze. Usually one of us does the check-in, and the rest of us wait on our bikes in the yard."

"So you don't always do the check-in?"

"It's a seniority thing. When I'm the top dog, I do the check-in. If someone on the escort team has been here longer than me, he does the check-in. It's just courtesy, not required."

"Was there a guard in the garage?"

"No. Just the Jacksons, the drivers."

"OK. Go on."

"Well, there's not much more to tell. I did the check-in. The armored pulled up. I double-checked the license plate against what had been on the manifest, which was a waste of time because I knew the two drivers, Harry and Charlie. The Jacksons were in the armored ready to go. I signed the manifest and left it on the desk inside the garage. I walked out of the garage, got on my bike, and we took off. Very routine."

"Did you know the other riders in the escort?"

"One of them well. Charlie, like I told you. He's a long-time employee. The other two were recent hires, college students, maybe been on board two years. Off and on."

"But everyone had ID?"

"Had to. Otherwise they would not have made it through the gate."

"Did the guard at the front gate stop you?"

"Nope. He just kind of waved as we went by."

"So you went out the gate. Where were you?"

"In the back. The two newbies were in front."

"The other long-term escort rider—Charlie, right?—was in the back with you?"

"Yup. Charlie and I were the two in the back."

Noonan picked up a file he had not yet reviewed. "Charlie Schanche, is he the long-timer?"

"Yes. The newbies were John and Ramon."

Noonan looked at the tags on the other two personnel files. "John Swensen and Ramon Delgado. Is John Swensen any relation to the owner of the company?"

"As far as I know, it's a yes-and-no answer. Old man Swensen—that is, President Swensen—was a foster child. He and his sister. President Swensen never married, so he has no children. His sister adopted a foster child., She give him the Swensen last name. To extend the family line, so to speak. That's John. Sharp, hardworking, honest. So, yes, there is a relationship, but, no, it's not blood."

"How about Ramon? Anything I should know about him?"

"Hispanic."

Noonan smiled. "That's a given."

"Not really. Bright kid, shows up on time, does the paperwork he's required to do. I've got no complaint with either of the newbies."

"How about the long-timer," Noonan looked at the personnel file tab, "Charlie Schanche?"

"Charlie is old school. Vietnam vet. Black Beret, and I'm not even sure what a Black Beret is. Was. Burned out, if you know what I mean. Had a rough life, rocky marriage, couple of kids who dropped out. Uses drugs. Prescription drugs, not illegal ones. He's alert enough on the job but just kind of there. Good enough for me to trust him."

"Never gave you any trouble?"

"None of these guys did. But none of them are my friends. We're just the luck of the draw. I'm with Charlie a lot because he's been here a long time. People come and go in this business."

"How about the two newbies? Ever work with them before?"

"A handful of times, yeah."

"Together or separately?"

"Both. Like I said, it's the luck of the draw."

"No problems with any of them?"

"Not a one. But like I said, these are people I work with. I don't party with them."

"How about the drivers?"

"I know them better because they've been around a long time. Harry and Charles Jackson. Same last name. Same family. Odd because they're not closely related. But then again, this is coastal North Carolina and the Outer Banks, so their family have been here a long time. Distantly related but related, if you know what I mean."

Noonan kind of nodded. Then he picked up the personnel files of the two Jacksons. "Harry and Charles." Noonan opened the Manila folders and looked at the contents. He took so long that Steigle started looking around as if to leave. Without looking up Noonan said, "This 'ill just take another minute or two." Then he put the files down.

"Both of these guys are in their upper sixties. Were they here when you were hired on?"

"Been here longer than rocks," Steigle said. "They were old-timers when I was a newbie."

"Are they full-time?"

"No one here is full-time. The longer you work here, the more you make per hour. They're up there in terms of per hour."

"Good money?"

"For not having a college degree, yeah. I don't know what good money is anymore. I made great money when I was a lawyer. But three wives leave you kind of broke."

"Three ex-wives, you mean."

"They all have kids, so I'm always paying."

"Anyone else here have money problems?"

"Captain," Steigle said confidentially. "It is captain, isn't it?"

"Heinz works better."

"Heinz, I know where you're going. Yeah, everyone who works here needs money. But there's a difference between needing money and dipping into the till. First, there is no till to rob here. Money in the vault is audited. When the cash goes into the armoreds, it's in locked bags. Paperwork is checked at the front end and back end. If there so much as a dime missing, we're all out of a job. Yeah, we all need money, but none of us can afford to steal it. Besides, we never see money; we just see bags of it. Or, what we think are bags full of it."

"How much money was in the armored when it disappeared?"

"None. We were on our way to pick up money."

"What do you think happened to the armored?"

"Don't have a clue. It went into the tunnel. We waited on our end. It never came out the other side. Never came out our side either."

"Let's do this a bit slower."

"OK. What do you want to know?"

"You went out the front gate. Then what?"

"Well, we proceeded toward the Pamlico Tunnel. When we got there—"

"Wait a minute. Did you have to change your route for any reason?"

"No. Not really."

"What do you mean by *not really*?"

"Well, there was a motorcycle that had been laid down. I didn't see it go down, but it was flat on the ground when we drove up. The rider was up and standing over the motorcycle. He didn't look hurt, so we just went around him."

"Did you drive around the motorcycle?"

"Sort of. We went around the block because a crowd was gathering in the intersection. But that was about it."

"You didn't stop?"

"There was no reason to. The rider was up and walking around. We just detoured around the block."

"Did you lose sight of the armored car at that point?"

"Heinz, we never lost sight of the armored car until we got to the tunnel. There were two motorcycles in the front and two in the back. The newbies in front, me and Charlie in the back. We were close enough to the truck bumper to touch it all the way to the tunnel."

"Were you going a normal rate of speed at all times?"

"A little slower than normal but not above the speed limit, which is pretty slow—twenty-five miles per hour in most places. Like I said, it was all routine."

"OK. What happened when you got to the tunnel?"

"Like I've told everyone before, the State of North Carolina was doing roadwork in the tunnel, so there was only one-way traffic. I sent two of the motorcycles, the newbies, on ahead to check out the tunnel and wait for the armored on the far side. They went through with a convoy."

"Convoy?"

"Yeah, you know, in a queue. There was construction in the tunnel, and three of the four lanes were closed. So the cars had to go through single file. The roadway was pretty ripped up in there, with huge potholes you had to maneuver around. Vehicles had to go in single file. There was a traffic control person on our side, who let six or seven cars go through at a time—vehicles, I mean. Traffic was moving real slow. Traffic woman—it was a woman—didn't want to jam up the tunnel, so we went through in convoys. When all the cars came out on the other side, the traffic guy on the other side of the tunnel let cars go in from the other direction. Then the traffic woman let the next plug of cars go through from our end."

"Were the two traffic people in contact with each other? Like on cell phones?"

"No. The last car in the convoy was given a flag. When the last car came out on the other side of the tunnel, the flag was given to the other traffic person, and he gave to the last car in the convoy coming the other way."

"So the newbies went through first?"

"Yes. They went through with a convoy. Then, when they got out on the other side, they sat and waited for the armored. The convoy coming our direction came through, and the last car gave the traffic woman the flag. She gave it to the armored, the last vehicle in the convoy on our side of the tunnel. Then Charlie and I waited for the armored to get through, but it never came out on the other side."

"Why did you wait rather than follow the armored?"

"Protocol. Even if it wasn't, it was not a good idea to be in the tunnel behind the armored. The potholes in the Pamlico Tunnel could drown an elephant."

"So the armored went in and never came out of the tunnel?"

"Never came out. The armored car went into the tunnel at the back of the convoy. It disappeared into the tunnel, and that was the last time Charlie and I saw it."

"OK. Now I'm assuming you made a thorough search of the tunnel, even in places an armored car couldn't be."

"Captain, we searched everywhere. We asked for a roadblock and chased down all the vehicles that came out of the tunnel on the other side. There's no turn-off on the highway, so it wasn't hard. There were only eight cars in the convoy, and none of them was the armored car. Two of them could have had the armored car inside, but we checked both. Then we walked back through the tunnel and found nothing."

"Nothing?" Noonan's look was incredulous. "I find it hard to believe."

"Captain, I'm telling you, there was nothing there. The armored car did not come out of the tunnel at the far side. It didn't back out of the tunnel; otherwise, Charlie and I would have seen it."

"Do you always split up your security when you come to a tunnel?"

"Not every tunnel. Just the ones where there is a chance of robbery. Traffic was moving very slowly because of the construction. It was deemed a good idea to take the precaution, and that's exactly what my men did. Now, of course, it doesn't seem like such a good idea."

"The tunnel only had one lane open, right?"

"The State of North Carolina is working on the tunnel, repaving it, so there was only one lane open. That's why the traffic inside was moving pretty slow. Two of our motorcycles went over in the first convoy. Then the armored car went through with eight other vehicles. When it didn't show up on the other side, one of the escorts, John, came back to see what the problem was. That's when we knew the armored was missing."

Noonan shook his head. "Could the armored car have turned around in the tunnel?"

"If the roadway was fixed, and it had time to do the old back-and-forth, yeah. But there was only one lane open, and even the one lane was pretty chewed up, anyway. They're paving in there."

"Was anyone in the tunnel?"

"No. The pavers were on lunch break."

"So they left the paving equipment in the tunnel?"

"I know what you're thinking, Chief. I thought the same thing. We checked all the equipment. It's all standard, and none of it is large enough to hide an armored car. We walked the tunnel four abreast with flashlights to make sure it wasn't parked against the side and covered with a tarp or hidden in a pullover. There was nothing there. Nothing."

"Were there any holes in the tunnel? Armored cars don't just disappear into thin air."

"This one may very well have. Yes, there are some holes, but I'd call them alleys. That's the only thing I can think to call them. They run about twenty feet and then connect with a hallway on the riverside of the tunnel. The alleys are there so water can be drained out of the tunnel. The back hallway's about five feet wide, but there's a four-foot-wide aqueduct running down the center. The aqueduct was full of water and had a grate over it. The water collects and then jets out into the river. Then it's a two-hundred-foot drop to the river."

"Yeah. Yeah. I saw *the fugitive*. And the vehicle wasn't there?"

"Couldn't get there. The alleys feeding off the tunnel are only about four feet wide, too narrow for an armored car."

"Are there any other openings?"

"Not a one."

"How about catwalks?"

"There are two walkways on both sides of the tunnel, but they are only three feet wide and have a railing. An armored car couldn't make it up to the walkway much less drive along it."

Noonan scratched his head and stared at the blank wall beside his desk. There was dead silence for a moment before he spoke again. "What about the police? You did call them?"

"They got there fast and were crawling all over us."

"Did the armored have a GPS?"

"Yup. But it went ghost on us."

"Ghost?"

"When we went back to the garage to report the missing armored, we checked its GPS. It wasn't on. Ghost. Our term, what we call it."

"So, in essence, the armored disappeared into thin air?"

"No *in essence* about it. It was gone."

Noonan kept writing as he spoke. "I'm assuming you did the usual. You checked to make sure there really was an armored car gone. I mean, you counted all the cars in the garage and searched every nook and cranny to make sure an armored wasn't hidden."

Steigle smiled and raised both hands to shoulder level. "This place may look large from the outside, but it's small on the inside, so to speak. We have twenty-three vehicles here; sixteen of them are what you call armored. The rest are what we call delivery vehicles. They don't carry cash. Yes, we checked every one of the twenty-two vehicles here and, as you call them, the 'nooks and crannies.' We were short of one armored car. We checked the security cameras, and, yes, the armored car left; it's GPS was active at that time. All the other armoreds had GPS working. There was one armored missing. It still is."

"With no money in it?"

"Not a dime."

"Who would want to steal an empty armored car?"

"That, Captain, is a very good question."

Chapter 8

For John Swensen, every day was a blessing. He almost had it all. True, he did not have a wife, but then, again, he did not have the problems a wife could bring. But he did have family.

He and his sister had been foster children, courtesy of a drunk driver back in the days when drunk drivers were grist for stand-up comics. They had been adopted by the same couple, so, at the very least, they had grown up together. She was sterile, so she and her husband had adopted a foster child, kind of a payback thank-you to the system that had saved her life.

Swensen himself had done well over the years. He had started out as a guard at the armored-car company he now owned. The company had doubled in size since then but was not in the league of the bigger companies in Virginia Beach, Richmond, or Wilmington. But he had a stable client base, mostly in the tourist-infested coastline and inland as deep as Vanceboro and Plymouth with a few irregular deliveries as far inland as Goldsboro and Tarboro. While he was not making much in net, he had a substantial nest egg in real estate. He owned the company, its warehouse, vault, and garage free and clear. He was wealthy in land and building, not cash. He didn't make much, but he didn't need much.

The one dark cloud in his existence was a prostate tumor. It was sleeping now, courtesy of a regime of chemo, and he was recovering his strength and stamina. He knew each day was a blessing and treated every day that way.

He had scheduled a meeting with his sister's adopted foster child for Monday morning. Then the armored car went missing on Sunday, and it had wiped his calendar clean. Now his day was clogged with troopers, insurance agents, and two distraught wives who wanted to know why their husbands had not come home from what was basically a cakewalk day in the armored-car business. Really, Sunday's run had been to collect money, not deliver it. And the armored had not collected a dime. So why was the armored missing?

Right after the troopers and insurance agent left his office, his foster nephew, John, came in with Ramon Delgado. They had been the two security bikers for the missing armored car, but it was not the reason Swensen had called them into his office.

"Come on in and shut the door," John Swensen said to the two men.

Ramon shut the door, and the two men sat down across the desk from John.

"Things are crazy around here today," John said, looking at the two. "But what I have to tell you might not be able to wait."

The two young men looked at each other and then back at John.

"I'm not going to pull any punches," John said. "It's not my style. You two know it. The two of you are gay, or whatever it's called these days, and I could care less. What I do care about is this company." He drummed his fingers on his desk. "I've just been through a regime of chemotherapy for prostate cancer and so far," he knocked on the desk, "it's in remission. As soon as this missing armored-car matter is finished, I'm going to be stepping back from managing the business. My sister, your mother," John said, indicating the young Swensen, "is going to be taking over ownership of the business. What that means is you," again he pointed to the young Swensen, "are going to be expected to expand your responsibilities here. I'm putting your name on the vault log-in, John. It's more responsibility, but I'm sure you can handle it."

Then John looked directly at Delgado. "You are as close to family as John is." John tilted his head at the young Swensen. "Depending on how the law will change regarding gays, the two of you may very well end up owning this business." John raised his hands and eyes and half-turned.

The young Swensen and Delgado started to say something, but John waved them off.

"There are going to be a lot of changes with this business. The delivery of money was not what it used to be. There is still going to be the need for some kind of an armored-car service but not like it was in the old days. But that's not going to be my problem. It will eventually be your problem." He pointed at them with both index fingers. "It's time for your generation to take an increasing responsibility here."

The two young men sat in stunned silence.

"I didn't know you had cancer," the young Swensen finally said.

"I don't," replied John. "Not anymore. But the beast is still alive inside. It's just slumbering. I'm going to be taking time off, immediately. That means the two of you are going to be moving up the corporate ladder here quickly. I've seen the two of you work. I'm not worried about the company. But I worry the details are going to overwhelm your mother." He pointed at the young Swensen.

There was embarrassed silence for a moment. Then John said, "That's all I have to say. Now I get to spend the rest of the day dealing with the troopers and insurance agents. The two of you had better be thinking about your future in a whole new manner. Now, I've had my say. Go out and plan your future; I'm working on mine."

The two young men rose to leave, but John waved them back into their chairs.

Smiling, he said, "You might as well start your corporate adventure with a mystery as well as a trial of fire." He picked up his phone and said, "Send Richiamo in."

Chapter 9

Lenny Rusnak was sitting in his lawyer's office with a spread of documents over the Oakwood desk.

"George." Rusnak was scratching his head. "I'm not a push-the-envelope kind of guy when it comes to the law."

"You should have thought about that before you got into the marijuana business," his lawyer told him with a sardonic smile. "It's one of those legal-illegal kinds of businesses." George looked like a lawyer. He talked like a lawyer. As far as Rusnak was concerned, everything was all good. He was being up and up. Rusnak did not need trouble with anyone. Particularly not the IRS. Even though he was selling a federally illegal but state-legal product, he did not dodge the tax man. Look what it got Al Capone.

"It's a legal-illegal business *now*," said Rusnak. "It won't be in five years. I look at myself as more of a frontiersman."

"Frontiersmen get killed by Indians."

"What a pleasant thought." Rusnak extended his hand over the paperwork spread on the lawyer's desk. "What do you think?"

"Honestly, it's workable." George gave a sniffle.

"Is it legal?"

"Yes. But you must understand this is what we legal beagles call an 'arm's length transaction.' In dollars-and-cents terms, you cannot put the money you make in a bank."

"The money I make legally by selling marijuana—*we*, actually. I do have partners."

"Yes. The money you and your partners make legally by selling marijuana is only legal in your stores. In the states where marijuana can legally be sold. If you try to put it in a bank, any bank in any city in any state of the United States—or territory, let me quickly add—it is illegal money."

"That's crazy."

"No, that's the law. Money from marijuana is drug money. The banks can't take drug money, and they cannot let you use banking instruments like checks, debit cards, or credit cards to buy marijuana."

"I know that. What I want to know is if this," he pointed to the legal documents on the desk, "is legal."

"I'll tell you the same thing I told you when you brought me these documents six months ago. This," he waved his hand over the desktop, "is legal. The paperwork is fine. Your money is fine. But the problem is finding a way to fund this investment with marijuana money. If you show up and just give these people cash, any bank they use is going to seize the money, the cash. Then you won't have the money, and you won't have the asset."

"So what you are saying is, we have to come up with a legal check for ten million dollars, which a bank will accept."

"Correct. And remember," the lawyer cut Lenny off, "don't buy off on this Bahamian bank noise. If you put the money in a Bahamian bank and then use a check from the Bahamian bank to pay for this asset," he waved his hand over the documents again, "it's called laundering. What you have to do is come up with a legal financial instrument you got with an arm's length transaction in the United States from an American bank."

"How do I go about doing that?"

"Don't ask me! I'm a lawyer, not a magician."

Chapter 10

Joseph Richiamo was his usual cheery self when he met with President Swensen in the office of the Swensen Armored Car Company. John Swensen waved him into an open chair and introduced him to young Swensen and Delgado.

John Swensen and Richiamo were a mutual admiration society with the two of them welded at the hip. For Swensen, his benefit was a substantial sum per month for the transportation, no questions asked, of a briefcase-size delivery of a pass-through item from somewhere in Colorado to a lawyer's office in Ocracoke. About once every three weeks, the Swensen Armored Car Company would pick up said package from another armored-car company loading facility in Tarboro and deliver it to the Sandersonville armored-car facility where, the next morning or soon thereafter, it would be transshipped to a law office in Ocracoke. It was always a transshipment. All President Swensen knew was his company was being paid very well to make sure the shipment passed through his territory with all due haste and no delay. Every few months a similar package would come from the other direction, and, in reverse, the Swensen Armored Car Company would transport it north and connect with another armored-car company that would take the cargo to a destination unknown, probably back to Colorado where the chain of deliveries began.

Richiamo also stored cash with the armored-car company under unusual terms and not similar to other banks and business. He used the armored-car facility as a holding vault but kept his cash separate from other Swensen clients. But it was the briefcase-sized shipments that made Swensen the money. Richiamo's cash-storage charges did not even cover the pro-rata electric bill of the Swensen Armored Car Company.

There was no reason for President Swensen to know what was in the Richiamo briefcases. He was not paid to care. The Richiamo deliveries were like other deliveries. Swensen's simply operated as a high-priced trucking operation. It did not own the shipments it carried. It did not open the shipments it carried. His armored cars just delivered property from one location to another in a steel vehicle watched over by men with weapons. Everything in the trucks was insured, so there was no risk of loss.

Everything, that is, except those regular shipments of a briefcase-sized delivery of a pass-through item. This cargo was insured for a dollar. The single-dollar figure was necessary because federal licensing law required all shipments be insured. The one-dollar figure kept the ICC happy and the Swensen Armored Car Company in compliance with the law.

Richiamo was basically a paper shipper. His company dealt in paper that had no intrinsic value. A land title, for instance, was just a sheet of paper asserting someone owned property. The actual title with all its signatures and stamps was necessary to complete a transaction. He was a paper mill. He moved paper to be signed and sealed. Then the actual documents would end up in some lawyer's office. Copies were fine but not definitive. Richiamo had the Swensen Armored Car Company transport originals, not copies.

Richiamo's arrival was not unexpected. But how the news of the missing armored car could have reached him so quickly was unknown.

"Joe," Swensen greeted Richiamo casually, "I see bad news travels fast."

Richiamo smiled pleasantly at John Swensen and then at the two young men in the office. "Well, you know how little birds are."

"You got here at the right time," Swensen said and introduced Richiamo to the two young men sitting in the president's office. "These are two of the men who were guarding the armored car when it went missing."

"Missing?" Richiamo was sarcastic. "*Missing?*"

"There is no evidence anything has been stolen," snapped Delgado. "Misplaced, yes. There is no evidence a crime has taken place."

"And who the blazes are you?" snapped Richiamo to the young man, a touch of irony in his voice.

Delgado gave as good as he got. "I am one of the men who was guarding the misplaced armored car. I and my partner," he indicated the second young man in the room, "were guarding the exit to the Pamlico Tunnel, the Pamlico City side. The armored car did not come out of the tunnel. We searched every vehicle leaving the tunnel"—he paused just long enough to cut off a snide statement everyone knew was coming out of Richiamo's mouth—"and we had the backing of the troopers and some local police. Every single vehicle that came out of the tunnel was searched and cleared by the police."

Richiamo softened a bit. "Well, then what happened to the armored car?"

"We don't know," the young Swensen cut in. "We," he indicated himself, Delgado, and his uncle, "were just talking about it."

President Swensen cut in. "Joe, this is a nephew of mine, John. He's learning the business from the bottom up. He was one of escorts of the missing, and I mean *missing*, not *stolen*, armored car. And this is Ramon Delgado. He was another of the escorts. These two were on the exit side of the tunnel." President Swensen shook his head sadly. "Everything they say has been backed up by the troopers." Swensen picked up a sheet of paper on his desk and handed it to Richiamo.

As Richiamo was reading the trooper's report, he said, "Well, whatever did happen, it was quite a hiccup in your delivery schedule."

"Correct. But this *hiccup*, as you call it, will not affect your shipment or your deposits, if that's what you are worried about."

"Worried?" Richiamo gave a perfect impression of Alfred E. Newman. He pointed at his face with the index finger of his right hand. "What, me worry? Concerned? Not really. Just cautious." Then he looked pointedly at the two young men.

"Cautious is our way of doing business," President Swensen assured him. "As to your most recent delivery, it is still in the lock-up here."

Swensen had no opinion when it came to anyone's shipments. Richiamo's were unusual, but then, again, the Swensen Armored Car Company took a lot of deliveries. Some were as small as a pack of cards, others the size of a steamer trunk. He never looked inside any of those deliveries. If a customer wanted a bank bag of valuables picked up at Point A on Monday and delivered to Point B on Thursday, the Swensen Armored Car Company obliged. No one looked inside any of the deliveries. No one could, either legally or physically. In most cases the keys and/or codes unlocking the deliveries were not in the possession of the Swensen Armored Car Company. There was no reason for the keys and/or codes to be in the possession of Swensen. Like a trucking company, the Swensen Armored Car Company just delivered goods; they did not own the goods they carried.

If Richiamo was a wise guy, as Swensen had mused when they first met, he was the strangest mafioso he had ever seen—in real life or on film. He looked more prey than predator. He stood all of five feet two and could have made a living as a Wally Cox impersonator. He never gave the impression of being well-rested and appeared as nothing more than a haggard, low-level accountant in some giant bank rather than, well, whatever it was he did from nine to five. And whatever that was, it did not involve being in the sunshine. While Colorado was famous for its outdoor activity, Richiamo had the pallor of the Pillsbury Doughboy.

John Swensen towered over Richiamo. Swensen had played basketball at the University of Nebraska, and even though it had been decades earlier, he had kept his athlete's physique with weights, group power, step aerobics, and watching his diet. Richiamo had a paunch, while Swensen had a dad-bod—in spite of the fact he had no family. John had a full head of hair; Richiamo not so much and was losing what was left.

Richiamo broke the momentary silence by asking to see the package.

"Seeing the package will not be a problem, Joe. John and Ramon can show you the package," he paused briefly, "but just to show it is still in the warehouse. Opening it will be a problem. Legally we, that is, the Swensen Armored Car Company, do not own any shipments, only the transportation of the shipments. We pick up and deliver shipments on contracts. We do not open them for any reason here in the shop."

"But I am the shipper," insisted Richiamo.

"True," responded Swensen. "I know that. You know that. But the paperwork lists RMD, LLC as the shipper. I can only legally allow a bona fide representative of RMD, LLC to take possession of the package early."

"But I am the *R* in RMD, LLC."

"I know that. You know that. But the ICC does not. And the insurance companies do not. To let you open the shipment, I need some paperwork from RMD, LLC. Legally, I cannot even tell you if the package is here. Even though it's yours, and I know it, and you know it. All I can legally do is assure you the package is in the holding facility. Besides, what difference does it make? Your shipment is going out tomorrow, and within a matter of hours you will know if the shipment is moving."

Richiamo smiled. "My concern is more than just this one shipment. I mean, if you can lose an armored car today, what about tomorrow?" The young Swensen and Delgado stood up suddenly, but President Swensen waved them back into their chairs.

"We haven't *lost* an armored car, Joe. It's been misplaced. I find it hard to believe an armored car—and particularly an empty one— can simply just up and disappear."

Richiamo smiled weakly. "Things do happen, and there is quite a lot riding on my shipments."

Swensen shook his head. "Joe, I can show you the shipment, but you cannot open it. By the time you got the legal paperwork to get it open here, it would already be in Ocracoke. Do you want me to hold the package here until you get the paperwork?"

Richiamo thought about it for a *long* moment. "No. I don't think so. I'll just wait for it to move on down the line."

Swensen gave a chamber-of-commerce smile. "Anything to accommodate."

Richiamo took a deep breath. Then he asked, "Chemo doing you justice?"

"Picking up weight and having a hard time sleeping, but other than that, I'm in remission."

"No rest for the wicked, eh?" Richiamo rose and extended his hand across the desk. "There will be another shipment as usual in about three weeks." He looked slyly at the young Swensen and Delgado "Assuming you find your misplaced armored car."

John Swensen smiled as he shook Richiamo's hand. "Oh, we'll find it all right. Armored cars don't just vaporize."

Richiamo looked at the two young men. "And you two keep a sharp eye on my shipments, hear?" The two young men said nothing, just visibly boiled.

Richiamo turned to go but then had a second thought. "Just out of curiosity, how much money was in the armored car that *hasn't* vaporized?"

Swensen shook his head. "The legal answer is 'I don't know.' Like I told you, we only deliver shipments. The real answer: none. It was on its way to pick up money, not deliver it. That's what makes it so odd. Why waylay an armored car with no money?"

"Ah," said Richiamo. "The world can be a very strange place." He gave an odd smile. "Just to calm my nerves, how many deliveries do you have in your holding facilities at any one time?"

"Depends." Swensen kind of shuffled through some papers on his desk. "And only because you are a customer who wants to know. We are not like a post office where deliveries come in, we sort them, and then they go out again. Basically, we have three different kinds of clients. One, like you, is a simple pick-up-and-deliver. A second kind is what we call a *combiner*. We could have ten or fifteen small companies who do business with a single bank. We don't deliver to the bank every day, so we accumulate the packages and deliver the packages unopened, maybe, once in a week. These businesses are too small to have sophisticated electronic links to the banks, so we have to physically deliver the actual cash and receipts to the bank. Larger businesses don't have to do that. Money, as in cash, from a large business is automatically electronically recorded on the bank's books. Legally, I guess you'd say, the cash moves from the customer to the bank in a nanosecond. We verify the actual amount when we count the money here. It's best that way. The companies want their money earning interest as fast as possible, and the banks want access to the money to lend it out as fast as possible. Everyone is happy with the arrangement."

"But I thought the banks wanted the cash every day. If I were a business, I'd want interest on my deposits every day."

Swensen smiled.

"Oh, you are so old school, Joe. You're not a cash shipper, so you don't understand money does not exist anymore. The moment a business—the kind large enough to use the Swensen Armored Car Company—gets money in any form—check, credit card, debit card, cash, whatever—the money is deposited directly into the business account in a bank. We handle the paperwork here. It doesn't make any difference where the paper is; the money value is immediately transferred electronically to the bank. The five dollars spent in a store immediately is five dollars in the business account at the bank even if the five dollars, the actual paper money, is not at the bank." He paused and pointed at the young Swensen. "This is a good discussion to have now because John and Ramon, here, need to know the nuts and bolts of what the Swensen Armored Car Company does. Otherwise I would have waved off the question," he said, smiling.

"But when does the bank get its money?" Richiamo now showed interest in the process. "I mean, the actual dollars, checks and debits."

"For the big companies, electronically the bank gets it right away. It doesn't make any difference if the money is in the form of cash, checks, credit cards, or debit cards. Once the money is transferred electronically, the paper called checks and card receipts is simply filed away here. It's just backup. The cash sits in our vault. Here. We count it and store it. Think of this part of our operation as a storage facility. We simply store paper with cash value the banks already have on their books electronically. Once every couple of months, we transport the actual paper to a bank's storage vault. Maybe. The money—as in cash—usually just sits here until it's needed. When a small business wants, say, ten thousand dollars in cash for the Fourth of July weekend, we take ten thousand dollars in cash out of the vault, debit the bank's record, and credit the small business."

"But when does the money, the actual pieces of paper, make it to the bank vault?"

"It rarely does. To the rest of the world we appear to be a money *movement* operation. In actual fact, we are a *cash holding* facility. We hold money—what you call cash—for the banks until such time as they want the cash, or it is shipped to the feds. No one wants cash anymore. It has to be counted, stored, protected. That's part of our service here at Swensen."

"But RMD, LLC has cash here."

"In your case, yes. We have a palette of RMD, LLC cash, which you have asked us to keep separate from the rest of the money, cash, in the vault. But other than being identifiable because it is on a palette, the process is the same. Your money comes into the vault, it is counted, and you get a receipt. But the money just sits in the vault. It's part of our inventory. The only difference is that we can point to the palette and say, 'That's RMC, LLC's cash.'"

"Forget the money. It's covered by insurance. I'm worried about my package. You just said I could not open my package," Richiamo started to protest.

"You cannot open your package because you are a transport client. We move your shipment; that's it. For the banks, we warehouse their money, so to speak. They can come and look at their money any time they want—the electronic record of the money, that is. They never do. But they can come any time to look at our money—cash, that is. But it's just paper in bundles in storage crates. It does not have anyone's name on it."

Richiamo started to speak, but Swensen politely cut him off. "You are thinking of money in terms of something you can hold in your hand. That's *cash*, and the only thing that matters is who owns the paper, not where the paper is. Once a twenty-dollar bill has been spent in a store, the store records the twenty-dollar sale electronically. The bank gets it as a credit right away."

"But it doesn't have the twenty-dollar bill."

"Correct. The bank doesn't need it. We do—for the businesses that use us, anyway. We verify the receipt of the twenty dollars just as if we were the bank. Then we inform the bank—electronically—that the twenty dollars has been received here, but the value of the paper is already on the bank's books. We're just backstopping . . . er . . . double-checking the bank's and the company's records."

John Swensen leaned forward and said to the young Swensen and Delgado, "This is important for you two to hear. When a business electronically deposits twenty dollars in its account in a bank, the bank knows twenty dollars is available to be loaned out. See, the bank wants its money as fast as possible so it can lend the twenty dollars out. It leverages the twenty dollars out. Crudely stated, twenty dollars is going to come in, so the bank can lend out two hundred dollars. Ten times as much. In loans. It doesn't matter where the twenty-dollar bill is, the actual piece of paper. Its value has already been transmitted."

Delgado seemed a bit confused. "But what happens to the actual twenty-dollar bill?"

"We store it here." John Swensen looked at Richiamo, swiveled in his chair, and pointed at his back wall. "Joe, behind this wall is a massive vault. It's where we keep what you call *cash*. We count it and sort it. As long as what we say *is in* the deliveries matches what the businesses and stores said *was in* the deliveries, there's no problem. When the bank wants cash, say for a big sales weekend or Black Friday, they order so much paper money from us, and we ship it out."

"So we are basically a bank vault." The young Swensen got the point.

"Sort of," his uncle said. "Except the money is not ours. We are just storing it for a bank or large business."

Delgado pointed at the back wall. "So there are millions of dollars in cash in there?"

"Millions. About twenty million dollars," John Swensen said. "Give or take. But don't get any ideas. We are audited regularly, and there are snap inspections. We have been doing this for thirty years and haven't lost even one dollar."

"But the actual cash is there, our cash, RMD, LLC cash?" Richiamo said, pointing to the wall.

"Yes, but there are six feet of steel between here and there. Then there are all kinds of auditors and security people nosing around."

"So no one can get sticky fingers, eh?" Richiamo gave an odd smile.

"Not and stay employed here," John said. "Which reminds me, I must get some more personnel files for the cops, the 'Bearded Holmes' guy. Then I have to talk with the local police. And more insurance people. It has not been a good day, Joe. Let me assure you your cargo is safe. It wasn't on the lost armored car."

"I hope not," Richiamo replied. "It would take a lot of time and effort to replace what's in the shipment."

"Your shipment was not lost," cut in the young Swensen. "Neither was the armored car. It's just been misplaced. We'll find it."

"Just don't misplace my shipment," Richiamo shot back.

Chapter 11

Gloria Jackson was at the tanning salon when she got the call. She was naked, on her back in the tanning bed, and had to take off her eye protector to look at the incoming number on the phone. When she saw the number, she was not happy. She jammed in her ear buds. "What's the matter with you?!" she snapped. "You can't stay low and quiet for a day or two?"

"Just wanted to check in, babe," said Charlie electronically. "I miss you, honey."

"Don't 'honey,' me," she snapped. "Everything's on the line here. Now, you've said you love me. OK, prove it by staying silent for another forty-eight hours. As soon as the plane leaves, we can celebrate. But right now, you stay low and off the phone."

"But, honey, I miss you!"

"Three days from now, we'll be together forever. Until then, get off the phone, and stay low."

Chapter 12

Noonan was writing up his interview with Steigle when there was a tepid knock on the breakroom door. Noonan said something that sounded liked like "yeah" or "come in," and in walked the thinnest man in the universe. To describe him as cadaverous would have been an overstatement.

"You're the insurance man," Noonan said, remembering the movable skeleton from the trio in John Swensen's office.

"That's right." The erect corpse gave a wicked smile, revealing missing front teeth. "Harry Sandusky of North Carolina Mutual Indemnity." He tried to hand Noonan another card, but the captain waved it off. "You never know when you'll need insurance, Captain."

"Heinz."

"Eh?"

"Heinz. I'm not a captain here. I'm just on loan from homeland security."

"Odd. What does homeland security have to do with a missing armored car?"

"That is such a good question I don't have an answer for it," snapped Noonan. "As far as insurance goes, I've got nothing to report."

"So you haven't solved the matter of the dematerializing armored car?"

"You flatter me, sir. But I like the term *dematerializing*. It's so much better than stolen, missing, vanished, or misplaced. But words aside, nope. I don't have a clue. Why are you here?"

"Well, the Swensen Armored Car Company—"

"I know that part," Noonan cut in. "Why are you talking with me. There is no claim."

"Well, you know, you know, you never know. Things like this have a tendency to—"

"You've had a *dematerializing* armored car before?" Noonan emphasized the term *dematerializing*.

"Well, no. It's just North Carolina Mutual Indemnity insures everything here. We just want to know what's going on."

"Nothing is going on right now," Noonan said as he stretched his arms out. "Right now, there is no crime. At best, or, in your world, worst, we are talking about a destroyed vehicle."

"But there are the drivers, and they have families."

"Probably. I don't know anything yet," Noonan said, pointing to the folders on his desk. "I haven't gotten to their personnel records yet." Then he scratched his beard and looked at Sandusky. "Why are you really here?"

"Well, you know, you know, I'm just—"

Noonan didn't let him finish. "Let me guess. The *dematerializing* armored car is the least of North Carolina Mutual Indemnity worries. So what's the big worry? I mean, why are you here?"

"Well, you see."

Noonan pulled out the business card he had been given earlier to check the man's name. "Harry." Noonan gave him a hard look. "Don't give me a song and dance. There's a big picture here. What is it?"

"Well, you know, you know . . ."

"Harry . . ." Noonan let the rest of the sentence hang. And hang it did. There was a *long* moment of silence. Noonan did not break it.

"Well, you know, you know . . ." Sandusky stalled. "It's about the cash."

"What cash? There's none missing." Noonan shook his head. "The armored car was empty."

"No. Not the cash in the armored car. In the vault." Sandusky pointed through the wall behind Noonan's back.

"This is an armored-car company, Harry. There is always money here. What does the money back there," Noonan pointed behind his back without looking, "have to do with a *dematerializing* armored car out there in the real world?"

"Money changes people, you know."

"Harry." Noonan was clearly trying to sort out the connection between the *dematerializing* armored car and the money in the armored-car vault. "Harry," he said again. "I am here to solve the problem of the dematerializing armored car. The armored car had no money in it. I can't tell you anything about the money in the vault because it was not in the armored car."

"Oh, I know that, you know . . . you know . . . but . . . you know . . . if you should come across any hint there might be a connection—"

Noonan didn't let him finish. "I will pick up the phone and give you a call. Yes. But until I find a connection, Harry, there is nothing I can tell you because I don't know anything."

"Well, when you know—"

"*If* I know there is a connection . . ." Noonan corrected him midsentence. "I will let you know right away. But until I know anything about the money in the vault, this is only a case of a *dematerializing* armored car."

This did not satisfy the living osteological specimen, but it was clear that was all he was going to get from Noonan.

"Well, I'll be around, you know, just in case."

"I'll keep that in mind," Noonan said, and he went back to the personnel files. "Please close the door on your way out."

Chapter 13

Richiamo waited until he was a good block away from Swensen Armored Car Company before tapping his cell phone open. He didn't wait for a response on the other end. When the ringing stopped, he simply said, "Chum sprinkled."

Chapter 14

"What a toot: RMD, LLC. Just a bunch of letters with nothin' behind them." The old man snickered as he sipped his coffee. His legs were soaked to the knees.

"Well, we're in with 'em whether we like it or not. We didn't plan this, you know. We're just playing someone else's game."

"Ain't no 'they' in RMD, LLC. It's a him. Number one, and no number two, three, or four. A post-office box and business card. Followed him out to his office. In his house. No one there but him."

"So what?"

"Don't care, Harry. Don't care. We've got a few dozen hours to go, and then we will be out and gone."

"With luck, the going's gonna be good."

"If you plan it right, you don't need luck."

"I'll take it if I can get it."

"Then stay off the blasted phone. We don't need to push our luck."

Chapter 15

"Captain Noonan?"

"That's me," Noonan said as he looked up from the personnel files. There were two men in the room, neither of whom looked remotely like armored-car drivers or security guards. They had a Cookie-Cutter look. Like government agents. "Let me guess, FBI."

They smiled.

In unison.

The kind of a smile federal agents practice in front of their mirror—false friendliness with no commitment.

"Nope. We've got more personality than their people." One of them, the older one (maybe?), pulled out a badge. "Treasury."

"Secret Service?"

"Nope. They went to the Department of Homeland Security in 2003. We're with Financials."

Noonan scratched his head and then smiled. "I've never heard of Financials. That's what you said, right?"

"Yes. Financials. Part of the FinCEN—Financial Crimes Enforcement Network in Revenue. We're the people who go after money laundering and financial crimes."

Noonan took a closer look at their badges. "Nothing personal, but I've never heard of your office."

"We're very low key," Cookie-Cutter one said. "It's our way. No theater."

Noonan gave him an avuncular look. "OK, what does this . . . this . . ." He stalled.

"FinCEN," Cookie-Cutter two said. "FinCEN."

"Fine. What does FinCEN have to do with this matter? There's no proof the armored car has been robbed. Where's the financial crime you are supposedly investigating?"

Neither of the men said anything.

"Ah," said Noonan. "The old FBI response. Say nothing. So you are leaving it up to me to guess what you want."

Again, there was a twin silence.

"Keeping you in the loop, I've got zip. I haven't had a chance to look over all the personnel files." He lifted one of them and showed it to the Cookie-Cutter twins. "All I know is an armored car is missing. *Dematerializing* is the term I'm going to use until I learn otherwise."

"We'd like to be kept informed." Cookie-Cutter one handed Noonan a card.

Noonan looked at the card. All it had was a phone number with a Washington D. C. area code.

"This is how you people do business?"

"We don't advertise," said Cookie-Cutter two. "Like I said, we're not into theater. When you have something to say, give us a call."

Noonan chuckled to himself. "Is there anything in particular you are interested in? As far as I know, the armored car wasn't carrying any cash. No checks, no credit-card stubs, nothing. It was empty."

There was a dead silence between the two Cookie-Cutters. Then number one said, "Just stay in touch."

And they left.

As they were headed out, Swensen came in with more personnel files. Swensen acknowledged the Cookie-Cutters with a sad nod.

"You know them?" Noonan indicated the disappearing pair with a nod of his head.

"Oh yeah," Swensen said as he shook his head sadly. "FinCEN. They're with Treasury. They are money-laundering investigators. Financial fraud kind of stuff."

"So they think you are laundering money?"

"Captain Noonan," Swensen added a fake surprise to his tone, "didn't you know? Every armored-car company in America is laundering money."

"What does any of this have to do with a dematerializing armored car? At best, it's a state crime. The Pamlico Tunnel is in North Carolina. So what's the fed's interest?"

Swensen smiled sadly. "I have three answers for you. One, I don't know. Two, I don't care. Three, I don't have anything to worry about. Every cent in the holding facility," he pointed to the wall behind Noonan and then repeated himself, "every cent in those accounts is in place, and I've got the audits to prove it. We don't launder money here; we store it."

"Then why are the feds here?"

Chapter 16

"Charlie, stay away from the window!"

"We've only been here a few hours, and I'm already going buggy."

Charlie let the curtain flop back vertical and flopped on his bed. The room was hardly palatial, but then, again, it was secluded. It was a weekly rental, and if you wanted to disappear in America during the summer, the Outer Banks of North Carolina was the place to be. Particularly if you reserved your week in Paradise the previous November. Nags Head was the best of those possible places to be. Small enough to be called a community, but with so many tourist on holiday, it was more like a city. No one remembered anyone between Memorial Day and Labor Day. The perfect place to hide in plain sight.

Even better, the rented apartment faced the dumpster at the edge of a parking lot for a restaurant. There wasn't even a slice of the ocean—or Pamlico Sound—in the distance. No "view of" in the rental book. So it rented cheaper. And was more secluded. They had bought a week's supply of food the day before they moved in, Saturday, and planned to hide out for the duration. The steaks were in a refrigerator along with some hot dogs and sliced salami. No ribs because they required barbequing. They were to stay indoors for a few days.

No reason to attract attention.

No beer either.

They could have all the beer they wanted in two days. Three at the most.

Then they were going to need a lot of suntan oil.

Chapter 17

"Captain Noonan?" The woman stood about five feet two, a good foot shorter than Noonan. Noonan looked up from his notes. He was about to say yes when the policewoman cut him off at the pass. "I've heard all the short jokes, so don't try."

Noonan smiled. "I've heard all the tall jokes, so don't you try. Heck of a way to start a conversation."

She smiled. "Being a cop and a short woman, you get all kinds of guff."

"Being tall and old, you get all kinds of guff too. I guess we'll both just have to do our job, eh?"

It brought a smile. "Chelsea Edison. From the Pamlico City Police Department. I've been assigned to the case. I'm the records person."

"Records, as in files or as in recording?"

"Oh, you are card, you are. Both, as a matter of fact, when it comes to crime. For this particular case I was asked to do background on all the players in this . . . this . . ."

"Matter," Noonan finished for her. "This matter. Well, let me thank you in advance. I need all the help I can get."

"Well, records I can give you. Help, sorry, not so much."

Noonan smiled. "And here I thought you were going to solve the whole case for me!"

"Right," she snapped. "I'm the Easter Bunny on the side."

"OK," Noonan said, smiling. "No more jokes. What do you have for me?"

"Not much. I did background and credit checks for all the major players, the president." She kind of turned sideways and gave her head a tilt as if pointing back toward Swensen's office. "The four security guards, the two drivers and guard on the front gate on Sunday."

"Why the guard?"

"He was on duty when the armored car went missing. There were only seven people on duty on Sunday."

Noonan thought about it for a moment and then asked, "Only seven? Four security men, two drivers, and the guard makes seven. No office staff?"

"Not on a Sunday. Or, rather, not that Sunday. The armored car was empty, so there was no need for office people. When the armored cars come back on Sundays, the pickups are just put in a deposit drawer in the vault wall. There is no reason for any office or vault staff to be there on Sunday."

"OK, I'll go with that. Tell me about the seven."

"Nothing important. No red flags. Nothing suspicious in terms of money. Not all of them have good credit ratings, but nothing stands out. The two drivers have the worst credit ratings and lots of bills but nothing big-time. All of them have car loans, and none of them are behind. The two Jacksons have some police reports but nothing serious."

"What kind of police reports?"

"Marijuana possession. Not sale, just possession. Small amounts. Too small to be selling, if you want to know. As you know, we don't spend a lot of time on users. These guys were users, not dealers."

"How long ago was that?"

"Couple of years ago. Nothing since. No DV. No DUI. These are basically good-citizen types."

OK, how about the president."

"Clean as a whistle. No priors, no parking tickets, no reports, good credit rating, owns his home and car."

"Goody for him. The guard?"

"Clean too. Mormon, if it makes any difference. Strong family man. Average credit rating. No reports and no priors. Is buying a house and car and is current on all payments."

"You are *not* making my job easy, you know that?"

"My heart is broken. The four guards are different. The two young ones, Ramon and John, have an odd police report. They popped up in a gay bar call five years ago. There had been a disturbance, and they were two of the witnesses."

"Witnesses? As in victims?"

"Not victims. Or suspects, anticipating your next question. It was officially listed as a disturbance. Today we'd call it a hate crime. A group of young men entered the bar and started yelling at the gays, calling them all kinds of nasty names."

"I can imagine."

"When the three men would not leave, the police were called. Before the police got there, well, you can guess what happened."

"Yeah. What was the upshot of it all?"

"Some trespassing charges. One assault, not either of your people, and a police report to back up an insurance claim of damage."

"In other words, everything just went away."

"You got it, Captain."

"Heinz, I'm Heinz."

"OK, Heinz. That's it for two of the security guards."

"Where was this hate crime, by the way?"

"Long way away. Chapel Hill."

"I should have guessed. College town."

"University town. A college is in a small town. Chapel Hill is big-time."

"OK. Which leaves two security guards."

"Here's where it gets interesting but, again, no red flags. Charlie Schanche is a highly decorated veteran. But he has medical problems, psychological problems. Nothing serious as long as he takes his meds. PTSD is the modern term for it, but he's a Vietnam vet. I guess your generation would call him 'burned out.'"

Noonan smiled. "When it comes to crime, there is no such thing as *my generation* or yours. People are people, and only the terms change. Any priors or outstandings?"

"Nope. He's clean as a whistle. Not even a traffic ticket. He has a poor credit rating but owns his own car and three motorcycles. All are old. Wife has an engineering degree and is an HVAC specialist for the school district. Been there over twenty years. She's clean too. One divorce for her, and it was amiable. Just paperwork and done."

"How long were the two of them married?"

"First marriage? Three years. Current marriage, if that's why you're asking, twenty-five years. No DV in North Carolina. Her credit rating is very good. She has a car in her name, and their house—which is paid off—is in a family trust."

"His family or hers?"

"Theirs."

"OK. And now Mr. Steigle."

"He's a peach. A lot of paperwork but, again, no read flags. No arrests, no priors, no DVs but lots and lots of divorce paperwork. Been married three times, and each of them ended in a nasty divorce. It's his kind of paperwork that makes my job enjoyable."

"Really?"

"Yeah, it shows me how lucky someone is to have a quality husband."

"Steigle is not a quality husband?"

"From the court records, nope. Or, from what his exes say on the record, he was not a good boy. A lot of affairs, humiliating wives in public, lying about finances, the usually bad-boy things."

"No violence?"

"None."

"How's his credit rating?"

"Good. Very good, as a matter of fact. Even with three ex-wives, he's doing well. He kept his finances separate from his exes. Had prenups."

"He was a lawyer. I'd expect that."

"He's still a lawyer, in the sense he keeps paying his bar fee. No complaints with the North Carolina Bar Association. He does a lot of pro bono work for them, living wills and other end-of-life stuff."

"Seems pretty clean to me."

"And rich. He's the big fish in this pond. Everyone else has modest savings. Steigle is at two million. Low credit-card bills. He isn't buying a home."

Noonan cut in with a smile, "But he's paying for three homes for his ex-wives."

"Nope. Paid them off. Had a home until a year ago, but sold it. I could not find a new mortgage, so he's got to be renting."

"So what you've got me is nothing spectacular."

"Sorry."

"Anything else?"

"Like what?"

"Anything unusual pop up?"

"I'm not sure what *unusual* means. The president is a coin collector, if that means anything. Schanche is a member of two American Legion clubs, and the two gays are active in the gay rights community. The Jacksons are related to everyone on the coast, and depending on how you want to draw the related-to lines on a Ancestry.com chart, they have sleazy, disreputable cousins and nephews as well as upstanding members of the community. Take your pick."

"Well, you can pick your friends, but you can't pick your family."

"That's not the way I heard the saying."

"It's generational. My generation is so old, our driver's licenses are written in hieroglyphics. Do you have time to do some more digging?"

"I don't know where else to dig."

"I'll help. Do any of the seven have a gym membership? Are all their cars and motorcycles current with regard to registration? Do any of them have a pilot's license? Are there any liens on any of their properties? Do they all have cell phones, and, particularly for the Jacksons, are those cell phones up and running? Do any of them have business licenses or are any of them in limited liability corporations? Do any of them have passports? Do any of them have anything to do with foam of any kind?"

"Foam? As in something frothing or as shipping material?"

"Either and any."

"OK. Anything else?"

"Just check with the Division of Elections and see if any of them vote or have signed any petitions in the last few years. And then the troopers have a list of the vehicles that were stopped and searched when the armored car went missing. One of those vehicles had something to do with the disappearance. See if any odd items pop up from the list."

Edison kept writing as she spoke. "This is an odd collection of questions."

"Well, this is an odd crime."

"I'll get on this today. Some answers I can get quickly. Do you want the answers as I get them or all at once?"

"All at once. But I must have what you can find by, say, ten a.m. tomorrow."

"Ten a.m. tomorrow? Do you know something I don't know?"

"Not really. My experience," Noonan gave him an avuncular look, "from my generation on the police force, has been such that matters like this have a tendency to wrap up pretty quickly. The armored car went missing on Sunday, and we're at Monday afternoon. Things like this do not hang fire for a week. I'm expecting something significant to happen soon, and when it does, I want to have as much information as I can get."

Edison closed her notebook. "Then I'll jump like a rabbit for you."

Noonan just smiled. "I'll be here, so I won't be hard to find."

Chapter 18

Curtis Jackson, his cousin Harold, and a distant Jackson from Vanceboro did not have any trouble meeting in private. They did it in public. When you met in private, there were all kinds of problems. There were revenue agents everywhere, *revenuers*, and the Jacksons hated them as much as their fathers and uncles had hated them in the days of prohibition. You just could not trust the government—the government men, anyway. They never got it right and were always stepping in where and when they weren't wanted.

Curtis did his family business in public. Usually at picnics. He'd heard the revenuers used bugs and wires. Well, they could load up his office and telephone all they wanted. He didn't do the real business over the phone, hard wire, or cell. He did it the old-fashioned way: nose to nose.

Curtis, Harold, and Jerome socialized as they filled paper plates with North Carolina fare. Curtis was a seafood man and preferred fish and crab. That is, any kind of fish and any kind of crab as long as it was not blue. Harold was a meat eater, and Jerome a phony vegan. Jerome was a vegan when his wife cooked but a voracious steak-and-potato man at lunch. Every lunch. The three men filled their respective plates and wandered off to a remote picnic table. They all popped a beer can and sat down.

"I like the sound of this, Curtis," Harold said as he bit into a pork rib. "But it's right on the edge of a real problem."

"Harold, every day in banking we're on the edge of a real problem. There just aren't any rules for banking anymore. Business is advancing faster than statutes. Our new, necessary practices don't fit the mold of an antiquated legal system."

Jerome Jackson from Vanceboro was of a different opinion. "Half of me says you are correct, Harold. But the other half of me says if we don't move ahead of the times, we are going to get left behind. We cannot just be up to snuff on what's happening; we have to be ahead of the power curve."

"Up to snuff! Power curve! It's all just hooey!" Harold was skeptical.

"OK, Harold. Let me give you a for instance. Do you remember the Y2K faux crisis?"

"Yeah."

"What a lot of people do not know is the United States Treasury had something like thirty planes full of cash sitting on runways around the country."

"Really? I didn't know that. Why?"

Jerome cleared his throat. "Because no one knew what Y2K was going to do with the money supply. No one knew what glitch was inadvertently built into the banking computer systems. If, for some reason, there was a major glitch in the electronics, the banking electronics, credit cards across the country might not be accepted. Checks might not clear because of the electronics, not because there was no money in the accounts."

"But nothing happened!"

"You're right. Nothing did happen. But the United States Department of the Treasury wasn't going to take a chance. Just in case the worse happened—just in case—it had plane loads of cash on runways in about thirty airports just in case something went wrong. The economy is a very fragile thing. One electronic glitch and there would be major problems from here to Alaska."

"But nothing happened!"

"OK, Jerome, let's try this another way. Right now, we've got a client with ten million dollars in cash. He wants to invest it, but he can't use a bank."

"This is marijuana money, isn't it?"

"Yes, it is. This client has ten million dollars of legal money. But it's cash. He's collecting it from sixty or seventy marijuana sales businesses in six states. The money was earned legally. What's illegal—and I mean illegal today—is having the banks touch it. We can't accept the money. We can't allow checks or credit cards or debit cards to buy marijuana. Until the federal government removes marijuana from the Schedule 1 list of dangerous drugs, the money is legal and, at the same time, illegal."

"Well, if we get involved with it, the feds are going to snag the money. Even if your client takes the money to the Bahamas, opens an account and then uses a check from the new account, it's still drug money. Worse, it's now laundered money."

"That's all true," Harold cut in. "We're on a frontier. We have to blaze trails."

Harold shook his head, and Jerome tapped him on the shoulder. "Harold, look at this from the point of view of the feds. What we cannot do is take money from the marijuana people. We cannot take money that has been washed, laundered, or whatever other term you want to use. The money must come from an untainted third source. It has to be an arm's length transaction. What Curtis is doing is establishing the third party. The marijuana money is going to buy out the four land collectives on the Outer Banks. It's nothing more than a paper transfer. The collectives are going to sell out for ten million dollars. We are going to negotiate the deal. We get our cut for standing in the middle and doing nothing more than transferring paper. After all is said and done, we're in the cat bird seat for construction loans, operation loans, whatever, the whole nine yards. There's a century of good money in this for us."

"You make it sound so simple. But if the feds—or the IRS—sniff so much as a whiff of any deal with marijuana money, they are going to look under every rock. Once they see a marijuana dollar bill, the money goes bye-bye, the deal goes bye-bye, and we are on the hook for laundering money."

"Exactly the point. This transaction would be illegal if it were less than an arm's length transaction. We can't take money directly, and we cannot take it indirectly. So we must come up with a better way. We let someone reputable, someone beyond repute, legally wash the money here in the United States and then use the clean government-approved money to consummate the deal."

"Great," Harold said. "How do we go about finding an uninterested third party?"

"As a matter of fact," Curtis said, looking over his shoulder, "I've already found one, and you will love how this is going to play out."

TUESDAY

Chapter 19

When the Cookie-Cutters came back on Tuesday, it was with a warrant.

Sort of.

But it was an odd warrant, even for the feds.

They walked right into President Swensen's office and dropped the sheet of paper on his desk. Swensen was on the phone at the time, but when he saw that the paper on his desk was a court order, he told the person on the other end of the line he had to go. He hung up the phone and read the court order.

"You have a warrant?" Swensen looked perplexed. "Let me get this right. You are bringing a financial crimes warrant to an armored-car business? Why? We move packages of money we do not see for clients. We hold cash for clients, but *they* have the paperwork—we don't. We just store the money, the cash. We don't own it. We get audited once a year for the cash, but all the other audits are for our client's records, and they do their own audit. You people are after big-time bad guys. Big-time financials, right?" Then he took a close look at the warrant. "You've got to be kidding me, right? This warrant is garbage. Even I know it's garbage, and I've never spent a day in court."

Cookie-Cutter one was unimpressed. "You can read the warrant. We want to see the financials for these three companies. We also want to see all the paperwork for RMD, LLC."

Swensen tried to ameliorate the situation. "Guys, you have come at a very bad time. We are missing an armored car, there is a captain of the Sandersonville Police Department working the case here in the building, we are loaded with men and women in blue wandering the premises, I've got annual cash auditors from the Treasury coming next week, and I'm up to my ears in clients who want to know if any of their money was on the truck that went missing."

Cookie-Cutter two was just as unimpressed as Cookie-Cutter one. "Well, if you do not want us to look at the records, we can just close you down until you change your mind."

Swensen gave the Cookie-Cutters a sour look. "You feds are all the same. Were you born jackasses, or did working for the feds make you that way?"

Neither of the Cookie-Cutter said anything.

Swensen pointed to a bank of filing cabinets along one wall of his office. "OK, these three companies," he said, pointing at the warrant, "have their paperwork there. Everything is alphabetic, so you should have no trouble finding what you need. If you have trouble with the alphabet, I'll get you a copy. But you are not going to find anything of interest there. Those companies regularly audit their own holdings and then turn the paperwork into state and fed regulators. So you'll be looking at paperwork you already have."

He paused for a moment. "RMD, LLC is not included in that filing system because it is not a long-term storage customer. We *could be* holding cash for RMD, LLC in the vault—and I *am not* saying we have any RMD, LLC money in the vault. But if we were holding RMD, LLC money in the vault, it would be in bulk. For a bulk customer, we count the money as it comes in to make sure what the client says is being deposited matches what is actually in the box or bag, for instance. Then we would put the money in a location in the vault. We would not mix it with money from banks, businesses, or other clients. When it comes to cash, the paperwork we have from a bulk customer is an amount matching the amount in the box. The bulk customer gets a receipt, but since the bulk customer is not a regular client, their paperwork would not be in those files." He pointed to the bank of file cabinets.

Swensen tapped the warrant with the index finger of his right hand. "But this warrant does not allow you to see any cash from any client in the vault. It just lets you see records. The RMD, LLC has no records in those file cabinets. All we have on paper for RMD, LLC are receipts. Those are not records." He pointed at the bank of files.

"RMD, LLC is not a regular customer. As far as records for RMD, LLC goes, we get shipments from them every three or four weeks, and we carry those shipments through our region and hand them off to another armored-car operation. We don't open up the packages."

"We do," snapped Cookie-Cutter one. "We want to see the most recent package."

Swensen picked up the warrant and reread it. "There is nothing in here about opening up a package. It just says records."

"The records are inside the delivery." Cookie-Cutter one gave an hyena-like smile.

"I don't know that," snapped Swensen. He thought about it for a moment. Slowly he looked at the Cookie-Cutters and then the bank of file cabinets. "You guys don't give a rat's patootie about those records." He pointed at the filing cabinet. "That's just a red herring. All you really want is the RMD, LLC delivery."

Neither of the Cookie-Cutters said anything. For a moment one of them made a slight motion as if he was going to look sideways. But he never finished the motion.

"What is it with you people? The Swensen Armored Car Company is up to its ears in cash we're holding for banks. We've got an army of auditors through here every three or four months to audit the paperwork the companies submitted themselves—and I don't know why. And you want to see what's in a delivery package we never opened?"

"The warrant says records, and we believe records are in the delivery owned by RMD, LLC."

"You guys are putting me in a real awkward position." Swensen shook his head. "If I say no, you close me down for a week. If I say yes, I lose a long-time customer."

"You have a copy of the warrant," Cookie-Cutter one said, pointing at the piece of paper on the desk.

"Oh, that will do wonders," snapped Swensen with a false sense of confidence. "Let's get this charade over." He stood up and then said, "Let me make the position of the Swensen Armored Car Company clear. If we open the shipment and find just records, you are authorized to examine those records." He pointed to the warrant on his desk. "But if you find any cash in any form—checks, credit-card slips, certificates of deposit, whatever—it stays here in our vault. Those items are not records; they are personal property. Your warrant only authorizes you to examine records, not cash in any form."

Neither of the Cookie-Cutters said anything.

Swensen rose from his desk and headed for the door, the Cookie-Cutters close behind him. As soon as he exited the room, he turned suddenly and pointed at the file cabinets. "Next time you try to fool an old man, do a better job of it, OK?"

Chapter 20

Noonan put down the personnel files of John Sanders and Ramon Delgado when they came into the room.

"Thanks for coming in on your day off," Noonan said. "I know you were grilled up one side and down the other yesterday. I'll try to be as quick as possible."

Neither man did more than grunt.

"I'm not going to lie to you. This is a very serious situation. So let's get right down to brass tacks." Noonan waved the two into a pair of chairs on the other side of the desk where he had now set up his investigative *office*. "Right now, all we have is a missing armored car. No crime has been committed, so, at this moment, there is no official investigation as far as the police are concerned. But . . ." He let the sentence hang.

Delgado snapped at him. "We had nothing to do with any disappearance. We were following procedures to the letter. We assisted the state troopers in the search for the armored car. We reported—"

Noonan held up a hand to cut Delgado off. "We are a long way from any reporting records. Now, I want to know what happened on the exit side of the Pamlico Tunnel."

"The armored car never came out of the tunnel," John Swensen said flatly. "That's all we know for sure."

"So I've heard." Noonan smiled. "Now, when the armored didn't come out the other side, you chased down all the vehicles that came through with the last convoy."

"That's right. Here's the list of vehicles." John Swensen handed him a list. "You will notice the signature of the state trooper on the bottom of the page. We worked with the state troopers. They verified there was no armored car in the last convoy and . . ." he kept talking even when Noonan tried to cut him off, "and . . . and after we checked every vehicle *with* the state troopers, we went back *with* the state troopers to the Pamlico Tunnel, and it was empty."

Noonan let him finish. Then Noonan looked over the list carefully. "Now you looked inside these two container trucks and the bus, right?" He tapped two names on the list.

"With the local police *and* the state troopers. The container trucks were full of boxes," Delgado cut in, "which we unloaded to make sure the boxes weren't hiding anything. The bus was full of people."

Noonan continued as if nothing was wrong. "Well, what we have left are three or four compact cars, a pickup truck, a milk delivery vehicle—I didn't know they had those anymore—and a Mercedes. You checked out the milk truck to make sure it wasn't the armored car in disguise, right?"

"We checked everyone out," John Swensen snapped.

"No other vehicles raced away?"

"The minute we knew the armored car was missing, we called the cops." Delgado's tone was professional.

John Swensen cut in quickly thereafter. "By cell phone and radio. They had a roadblock at the first intersection within a few minutes. That's where we caught up with all the cars from the convoy. There are no turnouts or side roads between the tunnel and the crossroads where the cops had the roadblock. The roadway was pretty torn up on the far side of the tunnel, so traffic was moving at a crawl. I know personally because we covered every inch of the road. On motorcycle and on foot. There is a mountainside along one curb and a two-hundred-foot drop to the river on the other."

"Then you walked the tunnel?"

"Both of us," said Delgado. "We went through the tunnel with a fine-tooth comb. We blocked both entrances and rode it. Then we walked it. Then we walked it with the police. We checked the walls, turnouts, and those side alleys. We tapped the walls and poked under the fresh pavement. The armored car wasn't there; period."

"Tell me about those alleys."

John Swensen let Delgado take the lead. "Well, when it rains, like it has been for the last few days, water rushes into the tunnel. It's been doing it for years. The pavement is put at an angle, so any water in the tunnel runs to the riverside. From there the water is funneled toward these alleys set every fifty or sixty feet along the wall. The water is then channeled back into a large aqueduct in a hallway that runs the length of the tunnel. Then there are three outlets where the water rushes out of the aqueduct and falls about two hundred feet to the river below."

"How wide are the alleys leading off the main tunnel?"

"Not wide enough to admit an armored car," John Swensen added. "I'd say they were four or five feet wide."

"The back hallway?"

"Eight or ten feet but the armored car could get there down the four-foot alleyway."

"How about the aqueduct in the back tunnel? How wide is it, and how deep do you think the water was?"

"Judging by the grates, I'd say it is four feet wide. I . . . we could see water rushing when I flashed my light down, but I couldn't tell how deep it was."

Noonan stood up and paced back and forth across the room. The two young men sat in the military-style metal chair without making a sound. When the silence became oppressive, the two men looked at each other. Delgado was about to say something when Noonan continued the conversation.

"Guys, when you went over the tunnel with the flash lights, did you check out the alleys carefully?"

"Absolutely," they both agreed. "We didn't think the armored could drive down there, but we knew we could be wrong. We examined each of the alleys carefully, checking for scrapes along the walls."

"Did you find any?"

"We found some fresh scrapes on the walls of one alley, but it was only in one spot." Delgado indicted a scrape about four feet long with his hands.

"Where?"

"On the leading edge of one of the alleys, where it joined the tunnel."

"Describe the scratches to me, precisely."

"There were four of them. We counted them and took pictures— on my phone." Delgado held up his phone. He paused for a moment while he found the photos he wanted and showed them to Noonan. "Two of them on each side of the alley. All of them were on both the alley side and the tunnel side of the brick wall like something had been braced there. They were parallel, with the top two being about six feet off the ground and the bottom two about three feet off the ground. Here's a picture of me standing next to the scrapes to show how high off the ground the scrapes were."

"Send those shots to me," Noonan said as he tapped the cursed satanic electronic beast of the devil incarnate in his vest pocket and gave Delgado the number to the Mephistophelian gadget.

"Did any of the other alleys have those marks?" Noonan tilted the phone sideways to get a long view.

"No. I checked," said Delgado.

Noonan looked and spoke to the young Swensen. "When the water leaves the back of this hallway," Noonan tapped the phone, "is it a straight drop to the river?"

"Pretty much so," the young Swensen replied. "It's a long way down."

"There's no mountainside directly below where the water exits the aqueduct?"

"Well, further down, yes. But it's a straight drop to the water below. I don't think the water hits the side of the mountain. The water arches out and falls directly into the river. Actually, I'm not sure. We weren't looking at the waterfall, just the alley where the scrapes were."

Noonan leaned over the personnel files on the desk, lost in thought. Then he looked from the young Swensen to Delgado. "Where was the armored car when it went into its convoy?"

Delgado responded. "At the very back. The last vehicle. By the book, sir. We operated right out of the book. If it's the last vehicle in and is going to be robbed, it gets civilians out of the line of fire. It's standard procedure. The traffic person was told that."

"Who talked to the traffic person?" Noonan asked.

"Well," the young Swensen cut in, "we didn't. We were on the other side of the Pamlico Tunnel. Charlie or George did. The drivers don't talk to anyone while they are en route. They keep their windows up. So, no, neither of us," he indicated himself and Delgado, "talked with the traffic guy, woman actually, on the other side of the tunnel. We went through with the convoy ahead of the one the armored car took. There we sat on the other side of the tunnel and waited for the armored car."

"And it never came," finished Delgado.

"Right. Right," said Noonan absentmindedly. "How many minutes were there between the time the armored left the other side of the tunnel and the first car from the oncoming convoy came out of the tunnel?"

"Oh, I don't know," said the young Swensen. "We weren't keeping track. We just assumed the armored car entered the Pamlico Tunnel on the far side. Then we waited. I'd say five or seven minutes. Not ten."

"When the armored car did not come through, one of you went back to check to see why?"

"Yeah, that was me," said the young Swensen.

"And you saw nothing in the tunnel?"

"No armored car, that's for sure."

"See anything unusual at all? People? Equipment?"

"Some highway equipment, but that's it."

"How many more minutes before you realized the armored car was missing?"

"About the same as the convoy coming through. Six minutes. No more."

Noonan was silent for a moment. Then he looked at the young Swensen. "Do you know what the configuration of the convoy was when it went into the tunnel?"

"Absolutely. I had to write it down for the troopers. The list is in the file there." He pointed to a file on Noonan's work desk.

"Did the convoy stop in the tunnel?"

"No one said it did. We talked to every one of the drivers of the vehicles who came out of the tunnel."

"Was there a truck in the original convoy?"

Delgado cut in. "When it came out of tunnel, yes. I wrote up all the information on vehicles for the troopers.

"What kind of a truck was it?"

"Large, a big one. One of those heavy four-wheelers with roll bars."

"What color was it?"

"Black and silver on the front and back, with red flames on the side panels."

"How high was the front bumper?"

"To my knee."

"Did you run a check on the truck?"

"Absolutely," said Delgado. "It was clean. No priors. Owned by a Yuppie in Garden Park."

"Did you actually look at his driver's license to check the face on the license with the face of the man?"

"Her. And yes, they matched."

"Did you check the face on the computer with the face of the woman?"

"Sure. I did it on the trooper computer. It was a match with the license she had."

"Was there any kind of foam anywhere?"

This took the two young men by surprise. Almost in unison they said, "Foam?"

"Foam," Noonan repeated. "Supposedly the drivers said they were being foamed."

"I . . ." Delgado started and then added, "we had not heard any reference to *foam*. All we, the two us, know is the armored entered the tunnel and never came out. I . . . we don't know anything about any foam."

Noonan pressed them. "So you didn't see any foam of any kind in the tunnel?"

Delgado looked at young Swensen and young Swensen looked back, both with question marks in their eyes. "Neither of us saw anything like foam. At least I didn't," he said. Then to young Swensen he said, "Did you?"

Young Swensen just shook his head and then said with a questioning face, "Foam?"

Noonan looked over the files on his desk and then looked up at young Swensen. "You're related to John Swensen, the president, correct?"

"Well . . ." young Swensen was hesitant. "Sort of. I'm the foster child of his sister. In that sense, yes, I am related."

"Are you being groomed to take over the business?"

Young Swensen started to protest but then said, "I guess you could say that. It's never been said to me in precisely those terms. John —that is, my uncle—has only said that as long as I work out, there will be a place for me here. He never said he was leaving the business to me, if that's what you mean. He's had some severe medical issues lately, and just recently he told me he is in the process of retiring. He specifically told me and Ramon," he pointed to Delgado, "we were going to be taking on a larger role in the company, but that's it."

"So you are not in his will or anything like that?"

"Not as far as I know." Young Swensen thought for a moment and then said, "I'm not stupid, Captain . . . Captain . . ."

"Noonan, but you call me Heinz."

"I'm not stupid, Heinz. Uncle John has no wife and children. His only blood relative is his sister, my mother. So, yeah, if something happens to him, then I will end up running the business, but my mom will probably own it. I guess you could call that motive."

"Motive?" Noonan gave him a strange look. "There has to be a crime for there to be a motive. Has a crime been committed?"

Delgado snapped, "Well, an armored car is missing."

"Missing is not a crime." Noonan looked at Delgado. "How long have you been working with the Swensen Armored Car Company?"

Delgado suddenly looked surprised. "I didn't make the armored vanish."

"I didn't say you did," Noonan responded. "I only asked how long you've been working here."

Delgado gave young Swensen a quick look. "About four years. John and I started together. When we were in college."

"So the two of you started to work here at the same time?"

Delgado looked at young Swensen and young Swensen looked at Noonan. "Look," he said, "it's no secret around the homestead.

Ramon and I are partners. We've been together since our junior year in college. So, yeah, we've been working here together for three, four years. I had the connection, and Uncle John doesn't care as long as we do a good job."

"He doesn't care you two are a couple?"

"He never said he cared. He treats Ramon like family at Thanksgiving and Christmas."

"Does he put the two of you together all the time? I mean, when you are at work, are the two of you paired up all the time?"

Delgado was quicker than young Swensen with a response. "Our lives together," he indicated young Swensen with a wave of his left hand, "is personal. When we work here, we're two employees. We're just like everyone else. When it comes to assignments, it's done randomly. That's the policy. Sometimes we work together, sometimes we don't. It's not like we are a team every time we show up."

"So you have worked with . . . with . . . with . . ." Noonan looked at the personnel file tabs, "Charlie and George from time to time?"

"Everyone works with everyone else from time to time," young Swensen snapped. "We don't know who is going to be working with whom when we show up. We arrive and get an assignment. I've worked with Charlie and George, individually and together. The armored drivers change too. I've worked with the two Jacksons before—again, individually and together."

"Was this last time any different?"

"Not really," Delgado said. "We arrived, and the guard at the front gate gave us the assignments. We got our bikes and waited for George in the lot. John and I were at the front. Charlie and George took up the rear. George went into the garage, checked out the armored, and came out. He gave the go-ahead, and we left." Delgado pointed to young Swensen. "We led the way, the armored followed, and Charlie was behind with George."

"Did you see them—I mean, Charlie and George—behind the armored car?"

This took the two young men by surprise. "No," said Delgado. "I mean, we didn't look to see if they were there. We just led the armored."

"We assumed they were there," cut in young Swensen. "I mean, where else would they be?"

Noonan didn't say anything. He picked up a yellow pad and looked at it for a moment. Then he asked, "What happened when you saw the motorcycle lying on the ground?"

"You mean the accident," Ramon said. "Nothing. It had already happened. The motorcycle was on the pavement, and a lot of people were standing around. We followed procedure. If there is an impediment, we are to take another route."

"You didn't stop?"

"We don't stop," replied young Swensen. "There was no reason to. No one was injured."

"No one you saw," Noonan corrected him.

"Correct," Delgado answered. "There was no reason for us to stop, so we didn't. We went around the block and were back on route in a matter of a few minutes."

"You didn't stop anywhere along the way, correct?"

"We didn't stop until we came to the Pamlico Tunnel."

"What happened then?"

"Well, we stopped then," Delgado said. "But it was the first time since leaving the Swensen facility."

"But you did stop?"

"Yes, sir," Delgado said.

"Heinz."

"Eh?"

"Heinz. My name."

"Oh yeah. Heinz. That was the first time we stopped."

"You pulled up to the tunnel entrance and stopped."

"Correct," Delgado said. "We stopped." He pointed to young Swensen. "The armored car was behind us. About four feet away. We talked with the traffic person and—"

"Did you know the tunnel was under construction?" Noonan asked.

"Sure," said young Swensen. "They've been working on it for weeks. We knew the convoy procedure weeks ago."

"So the process of getting through the tunnel was not new?"

"Nope," said Delgado. "It was set standard. We'd been through before. Old hat."

"So you didn't have to instruct the traffic person about how you were going to go through the tunnel."

"We'd been through the tunnel before with the woman. She wasn't new. She knew our procedure."

"Are you sure?"

"Absolutely," said young Swensen. "Besides, we told her again. Procedure. She did the 'yeah, yeah, yeah,' and Ramon and I went through."

"Nothing unusual about the day?"

"Not a thing," said young Swensen.

"Then what happened?"

"Nothing. I mean nothing unusual. We didn't know anything had gone wrong until the convoy came out of the tunnel with no armored car."

"How did you know the armored car had not been sidelined for another convoy?"

"We didn't." Delgado shook his head. "We assumed it had been because it had not come out with the convoy. When the armored didn't come out on our side, John," he indicated the young Swensen, "rode in the convoy going back through the other way, I mean, back from our side of the tunnel. He wanted to see what had happened. When he got to the other side, Charlie and George did a 'what's going on here?' That's when we knew something had gone wrong. We put in a call to the troopers and chased down the vehicles in the convoy."

"You stopped every vehicle that had been in the convoy?"

"Every one. There was no way for any of the vehicles to get off the highway. There was no exit, and they were moving slow because the roadway was torn up pretty bad. The troopers put up a roadblock in a matter of minutes and stopped everyone."

"When did you go back through the tunnel?"

Young Swensen cut it. "We didn't go together as a team the first time. I blasted ahead to make contact with the troopers. Ramon and Charlie went back into the tunnel."

"Where was George?"

"He went with me to the trooper blockade," young Swensen said. "It was all following procedure."

"The procedure is for you to split up your team?"

"That I do not know," young Swensen said. "It seemed the right thing to do. Actually, it's what George ordered us to do. He was lead. He just pointed at Ramon and Charlie and ordered them to check the tunnel. Then George and I headed for the trooper blockade."

Delgado followed up with "Later, when we regrouped, then John and George went through the tunnel. After that, all of us, all four of us, went through the tunnel."

"On foot?" Noonan asked.

"We've been through the tunnel on motorcycles, on foot, and with troopers. More than once." Delgado shook his head sadly. "There was nothing there. No armored car."

"What about the trooper blockade? Did they check every vehicle?"

"Inside, outside, up, and down," young Swensen said. "They matched every name and every plate and every license."

"And there was zip?" Noonan asked.

"Goose egg," said Delgado.

Chapter 21

It was not hard to break open the briefcase-sized delivery item from RMD, LLC. The Cookie-Cutters came with their own set of skeleton keys—or what passed for skeleton keys in the modern day and age. Opening the item was not hard. The Cookie-Cutters did something so quickly that John Swensen could not follow the action. He put the briefcase on a shelf in a storage locker next to the vault, and in the next instant, it was open.

"Just a second," he snapped at the Cookie-Cutters. "I need to get any money, as in cash, out of there."

One of the Cookie-Cutters tipped the briefcase forward. Dockets fell out on the shelf. But no cash.

"What are you looking for?" Swensen asked as the Cookie-Cutters piled the dockets on the shelf.

"Illegal financial transactions," one of the men said as he opened one of the dockets.

Swensen pointed to one of the open dockets. "Hey," he said. "I'm only half as stupid as I look. Those are legal documents. They've been filed with a court. Even I can see the stamps."

"Oh, they all are legal documents," said one of the Cookie-Cutters. "We just want to see the bulk of them in one location."

Swensen picked up the warrant. "It doesn't say anything here about legal records." He looked up. "This is bat poop crazy! You got a warrant to open a briefcase full of legal documents and you knew they were legal documents?!"

"Ah," said one of the Cookie-Cutters. "The United States government works in strange ways."

"Maybe so from your side of the table," Swensen said angrily. "But not here. Those are legal documents and your warrant," he shook the piece of paper, "just says you want to examine them. So they stay here. I have no reason to release documents that I believe to be legal."

"Oh," the second Cookie-Cutter said, smiling, "we're not going to take the documents. We're only going to photocopy them."

"You are going to photocopy publicly available legal documents? That makes no sense at all!"

"Like I said," Cookie-Cutter two said, "the government works in strange ways."

"Strange or not, I've got the Swensen Armored Car Company's reputation to consider. I've got to tell RMD, LLC their privacy has been violated."

The statement brought an unexpected response from the Cookie-Cutters. Rather than a snippy response couched in governmentese, it was a cautionary note. "You shouldn't do that."

"Really? Why not?"

"Because there is a lot more here than meets the eye. You said RMD, LLC stores money here. Money as in cash? In the vault? In cash form?"

"I never said that. And you don't have a warrant to ask that. If you want to know, get a warrant."

"I take that as a yes," one of the Cookie-Cutters said.

"All cash stored here is logged in, recorded, stored, and insured. We have not failed a single audit in the past twenty-six years. If any of the money, the cash, was from an illegal source, it would have been discovered by now."

"Well, you know . . ." started Cookie-Cutter one.

Swensen cut him off. "Look, what we have here is a real problem. Your warrant says you want to see records. You've seen them. The warrant says nothing about copying any records. And it doesn't say anything about taking them away. This is the dumbest search I have ever heard of. First, you want to open a private company's briefcase and look at documents you knew were public. Then you want to copy the public documents and put them back in the briefcase. Then you want to know about money stored here by the same company, without a warrant. What am I missing here?"

"Well . . ." Cookie-Cutter one started again. Before he continued he looked at his partner, who gave him a slow nod. "It's a complicated situation."

"No, it's not," complained Swensen. "Now you two come clean, or my lawyer gets involved, and I tell RMD, LLC the feds are looking into their packages."

"Well . . ." said Cookie-Cutter two. "Let's see what I can tell you without violating any confidentiality."

"Uh-huh." Swensen did not have a genuine scintilla in his "Uh-huh."

"RMD, LLC is actually involved in the drug business."

"Drug business? With legal documents?! Give me a break."

"The drug in this case is marijuana. You see, while marijuana may be legal in some states, it is still a Schedule 1 drug along with heroin and LSD."

"But RMD, LLC isn't shipping marijuana," Swensen said, pointing at the dockets. "That doesn't look like marijuana to me. Even if there was marijuana in the briefcase, it would be a state crime, not a federal one."

"Oh, there isn't any marijuana here. This is drug money being laundered."

"Give me a break. What you're telling me is RMD, LLC is *laundering* money from marijuana sales that were made legally."

"Not in this state." Cookie-Cutter one was striving for some justification.

Suddenly it dawned on Swensen. "Ah, let me see if I've got this right. What you are saying is, the RMD, LLC is taking money, cash, from legal marijuana sales in *other* states and moving it to North Carolina."

"Sort of," said Cookie-Cutter two.

"There's no *sort of* about it." Swensen was now angry. "Money from legal marijuana sales is legal money. It's not illegal money. Read your United States Constitution. It's called the Full Faith and Credit clause."

"True," Cookie-Cutter two broke in. "But money from and associated with marijuana sales is still considered drug money by the federal government."

"That may be true," Swensen cut it. "But it's garbage. Come on! Money from a legitimate sale is legal money. Even when it crosses a state border."

"True," Cookie-Cutter one added. "But as far as the United States government is concerned, it's drug money. It can't be deposited in a bank. And you can't use checks, credit cards, or debit cards to buy it."

"I know that," snapped Swensen as he pointed at the open briefcase with the dockets. "Those are legal documents." Suddenly his eyes popped with understanding. "So RMD, LLC can't use the United States Postal Service, can it?"

The two Cookie-Cutters looked at each other and then at Swensen.

"So, that's the game! RMD, LLC can't use the post office. If it did, you could take a look-see with no problems. But RMD, LLC is not using the post office, so you have to find another way to see the documents. Why not just go to state courts? All of those documents have been legally filed."

"Well," Cookie-Cutter two said sheepishly, "we don't want to tip our hand."

"Bat poop. You are doing an end-around-run. You don't know what RMD, LLC is doing with its money, so you want a peek at the other guy's cards. To look at all of the documents in one place rather than guess which courts in which states have the documents, you need to examine."

"Well, that's not exactly—"

Swensen cut him off. "This conversation is over. Now Swensen Armored Car Company has met and exceeded its obligation to the United States Government. You have looked inside the package as the warrant allows. There is nothing in this warrant about photocopying . . ." Swensen pointed to the sheet of paper on the shelf.

"It's reasonable to assume—"

Swensen cut him off again. He picked up the warrant and shook it at the two Cookie-Cutters. "I'm betting this is a freelance operation. You figured to buffalo me with paperwork. Wrong! You boys don't need a warrant to see any of the files in the other room. Those files are all from federally insured institutions. But you do need a warrant to see what RMD, LLC is doing with legal money.

I think this look-and-see is just a way to see if I will spill the beans and say RMD, LLC has money here and what it's going to be used for. All these documents," he pointed at the briefcase, "are public documents, and if you *don't already* have copies, then you are one sad team of investigators. No," Swensen stopped Cookie-Cutter one from breaking into the conversation. "No. The real point of this little, little exercise," he said, pointing at the briefcase, "has nothing to do with files and everything to do with cash. I can't legally tell you if RMD, LLC has cash here. You'll have to get a warrant to find that out. I'm betting you can't get a warrant because you have diddly when it comes to proof that RMD, LLC is laundering money. Even if RMD, LLC had millions here, it's legal money. The only thing RMD, LLC cannot do is run it through a bank. Until then, you're all bluff. Get the blue blazes out of my company, and don't come back unless you have a real warrant."

Chapter 22

"Foam?" Charlie Schanche gave Noonan a strange look as though he wasn't sure of what he heard. "You mean like Styrofoam?"

"Or car-wash foam. Anything that would have looked like foam anywhere along your route."

Schanche looked like exactly what he was: a burned-out Vietnam vet. He wore a badly beaten green military-issue jacket with a frayed collar and cuffs, faded jeans, and combat boots. The jacket had a POW-MIA patch on the shoulder of one sleeve, an Air CAV patch on the other, and a faded American flag on the right breast. His gray hair was pulled back in a ponytail, and he had crow's feet deep enough to mine coal. His hands were gnarled like those of a workman, and he smoked cigarettes so fast he was lighting the new one with the smoldering butt of the old. He was wearing a baseball cap with the words *Vietnam Vet* across the front.

Schanche thought for a moment. "No. I can't remember anything even looking like foam. There was a lot of water in the tunnel, and there were some bubbles on the surface but nothing like foam. Is it important?"

"Maybe. Maybe not." Noonan said as he wrote the comment in his notebook. "You're a vet, aren't you?"

Schanche smiled and indicated his baseball cap. "Hard to tell, eh?"

"How many tours?"

"Six in Vietnam, one in Cambodia."

"Cambodia? We weren't fighting in Cambodia." Noonan gave him a puzzled look.

Schanche gave a wry smile. "We weren't fighting in a lot of places I've been."

"No doubt." Noonan smiled. "How long have you been working for Swensen?"

"Oh, off and on for eight, nine years. I come and go."

"Nothing permanent. I mean, is this a part-time job?"

"Part-time for some, full-time for me. That is, it's the only job where I'm working consistently. I do some contract mechanical work sometimes—cars, trucks, engines, you know. Hands-on."

"Been riding a bike long?"

"Grew upon an Indian. Yeah, I'd say so."

"Now, the day the armored car went missing, you were bringing up the rear?"

"Yeah, back-end duty."

"When you got to work, did you go into the garage at all?"

"Well, sure, we all did. Had to get the bikes."

"So you and the others went into the garage and got the bikes. Then what?"

"Well, George was lead. He did the check-in. The rest of us—me and John and Ramon—got on our bikes and waited in the yard. Armored came out with George behind it. We took off. Simple."

"How long have you worked with George?"

"Three to four years."

"So you've been working at Swensen longer than he has."

"Pretty much so."

"Well, if you've been working longer than George, why didn't you do the check-in?"

"Didn't want to. Too much responsibility. I'm happy on the bike. He wants to do the check-in, fine with me."

"Was the decision made there in the yard?"

"Naw. Always been that way. Whenever we're together, George and me, he does the check-in."

"I thought the assignments were random."

"They are. Sometimes I'm with George. Sometimes I with Ramon or John or any of the others. I don't like to do the check-ins, so I don't."

"Do the others mind you not doing the check-in?"

"No. They get an extra buck and a half an hour for being in charge."

"You don't mind if they get paid more?"

"Nope. I'm happy with the ride and no responsibility."

"What kind of responsibility are we talking about?"

"Most of the time, not much. Look at the route on the city map. Check the invoice with the license plate of the armored, pull on the back door to make sure it's locked, wave to the drivers. That's about it. Nothing ever happens. It's all routine."

"Well, something happened this time."

"Luck of the draw. But it wasn't a robbery. The armored just went missing."

"It wasn't a robbery?"

"Nothing stolen. Even if it was, the money's insured. No one loses in this business."

"Any reason to think the drivers were involved?"

"Not really. Charlie and Harry have been with the company longer than me. Started with old man Swensen, I mean, John, back in the days of dirt. If they were gonna do any robbing—and that's what you're thinking, right? —if they were gonna do any robbing, they'd have done it long ago. And with money in the armored. The missing armored didn't have any money inside."

"How do you know there wasn't any money in the armored?"

"Because of the route. We were going to the mall to make pickups. Runs like that we don't have money in the armored because we're picking it up."

"So the armored was empty?"

"As far as I know. No reason for any money to be in the armored. Like I said, we were picking up money, not dropping it off."

Chapter 23

Curtis Jackson was going to be taking a busman's holiday. He hated busman's holidays. That's why he never took one. If you were going to have a holiday, make it a vacation. A West Coast vacation. A vacation where you went to a place you had never been and always wanted to go to for one or two fun-filled weeks. You jammed every bit of pleasure you could into those eleven days—with a day and a half of travel on either side of the eleven days.

But not this year.

Not this week.

It was a banking conference on Maui, as far as he could get from North Carolina and still speak English. He was going to be Schultz from HOGAN'S HEROES. He didn't see anything, he didn't hear anything, he didn't know anything. He'd have a perfect alibi; eleven days in Maui with lots of receipts to prove he'd never been off the Big Island. Maui was the Big Island, wasn't it? If not, he didn't care. He was just going to be a long way from North Carolina when the strange things were going to happen.

Tuesday night he had dinner at the airport in Virginia Beach. He had a debit-card receipt to prove it. Then he went through Security with his passport. Once inside the airport, he took a cell-phone picture of his boarding pass and e-mailed it to his office. He bought a Scotch on board and kept the receipt. By the time he got back from Maui, no one was going to doubt he had been far, far away from North Carolina for the week when everything had gone into a basket of spiders.

Chapter 24

"The bait's been taken. All parties are moving in our direction."

"It's about time. We are on a tight time schedule. This has got to work."

"Relax. The bankers are on board. The cops are busy looking for an armored car that doesn't exist, and the feds are being snookered by their own rules. We only need the feds to make one last stupid move, and we will be in the clear and long gone before anyone knows what's what."

Chapter 25

Noonan did not expect to find anything in the Pamlico Tunnel. He didn't find anything, so he was not disappointed. There was nothing to find. It was exactly what everyone described it as: a tunnel. Yes, there was ongoing construction work. Yes, it required a convoy to get through. Yes, there were side alleys where someone could hide but were not large enough to hide an armored car. Yes, both sides were controlled by traffic personnel. No, no one had seen the armored car. No, there had not been strange or suspicious activity before or after the disappearance of the armored car. No, no one had any theories as to how an armored car could disappear in a tunnel. No, there had been no foam of any kind in the tunnel.

Armed with his cell phone, measuring tape, and notebook, Noonan started at one entrance of the tunnel and lock-stepped his way to the opposing entrance. Then he did the same thing from the other side of the traffic pattern. He examined all the so-called alleys and niches in the tunnel, on both sides, and took a special interest in the drainage system. The widest alley was barely four feet wide, clearly not wide enough for an armored car, and it had a three-foot-wide storm drain running down the center of the alley. There was removable grate on the top of the trench-like storm drain. The trench was built at an angle so water could course out of the tunnel. The alley ran about ten yards before it opened onto an overlook. From there it was a drop of about two hundred feet to a pool of water below. There was a railing at the overlook to keep anyone from slipping into oblivion. The mountainside from the overlook upward was a sheer cliff. On both sides of the overlook, the ground was ankle-deep in mud with no sign it had been disturbed.

Noonan retraced his steps until he found the scrapes the guards had mentioned. There were three sets on each side of one of the alleys. The scratches were long parallel lines just like the security men had told him. Noonan measured them. He wrote in his notebook they were five feet long and separated by eighteen inches. There were some vertical scars above the parallel lines that ran to the ceiling of the alleyway. Noonan could not reach the ceiling, but he could see scrap marks along the edges of the I-beam running down the center of the alley.

While Noonan could not find anything to raise himself to the level of the I-beam, thanks to the miracle of modern technology—albeit courtesy of the cursed tool of Satan—he could zoom in on the I-beam from several angles with his cell phone. The resulting pictures were not "most excellent" as the younger generation would say, but as Noonan's generation did say, the electronic photos were "adequate, interesting, and useful." As Noonan was inwardly smiling about how the advance of technology was making the job of the crime fighter easier and more productive, the curse of the same technology began pulsating in his hand.

Evil incarnate was on the phone.

"Captain, it's so good for you to take my call."

Noonan rolled his eyes. Then he said nothing because, quite frankly, there was nothing he felt he could say without risking an administrative court martial. When the moment of silence became oppressive, the Sandersonville Commissioner of Homeland Security Edward Paul Lizzard III continued as Noonan waited with bated breath for the inevitable royal command.

"You are hard at work on the armored car thing, right?"

"That is correct, Commissioner. The non-crime investigation you ordered." Short was always best with Lizzard. The boom was coming, so Noonan held his breath. What bizarre request was about to be delivered over the demon of electronic origin?

"A matter of national security has come up, and I . . . we need your unique assistance at this moment."

Noonan held his breath; the curtain for the theater of the absurd was about to be raised.

"The Department of Homeland Security has been entrusted with a unique but time-sensitive task here in Sandersonville. It is a small task; I am sure you can handle in a matter of moments seeing you are in situ at the moment."

"In situ," Noonan mouthed nonchalantly, wondering if Lizzard even knew what the term meant.

"You know, in place, so to speak. You are working for the Swensen Armored Car Company, and a matter of national security has arisen involving the company. It's all hush-hush, you know. Undercover and all."

Noonan rolled his eyes. "Well, I see. What is it, exactly, you want me to do?"

"This is all secret, Captain, so you are to keep this matter close to your vest pocket."

Vest pocket? thought Noonan. *Where did that come from?*

"The United States Department of Revenue, Financial Division, part of the FinCEN, Financial Crimes Enforcement Network in Revenue, needs our assistance."

Here it comes!

"I . . . we have been asked to verify some moneys in the possession of the Swensen Armored Car Company vault. The money is not to be seized, moved, or sequestered; just examined to the extent it is there. And how much is there. Am I being clear?"

Lizzard was clear, but Noonan was not about to let the commissioner off the book so easily. "Sequestered? The money is not to be sequestered? What exactly does the Financial Division expect me to do? I mean, am I to count the money? I can't count the money without sequestering it. That is, I can't walk into a vault and be told five million dollars of all the money on a shelf is from one customer. Money is in a vault, not in boxes, per se. The vault of the armored-car company is like a bank vault. All the money is in piles, boxes, or bags by denomination. There is no way to tell which specific one hundred dollar bill came from one business and which twenty dollar came from another."

Lizzard sounded exasperated.

"Let me put it another way, Captain. FinCEN knows there is a certain amount of cash owned by a specific company that uses the

Swensen Armored Car Company. It assumes the cash is being held in situ in the vault of the Sanders Armored Car Company. All you have to do is look at the vault records of the company in question and see if there is an outstanding amount of money in the form of cash listed as being held by this company. Then you walk into the vault and make sure there is at least the same amount of cash in the vault listed as owned by the company. Simple."

Here comes the kicker, Noonan thought as he asked, "Will I have a warrant?"

"Captain, this is all very hush-hush. National security and all. We don't want the bad people to know we're looking at their money. Use your charm."

"Who are the bad people in this case?"

"No need for you to worry about it, Captain. You will be met at the armored-car company by two FinCEN agents."

"Will they have a warrant?"

"Hush-hush, Captain. This is all hush-hush." Before Noonan could respond, his cell phone went ghost.

Chapter 26

"Bait taken."

"Assemble the team. We want to be long gone by the time the sun comes up."

"Plan in place. Hotel reservations made."

Chapter 27

One thing about Harry Sandusky: every time you figured you'd seen the last of him, poof, there he was again. He was like a bad penny. This time he came with friends.

"What is it, Harry?" John Swensen said as he looked up at the cadaverous insurance representative. Sandusky was not alone. He was with three men who pulsed accountant. They were all dressed in ill-fitting black suits with white shirts and dark-blue ties. They all had jacket breast pockets filled with pens. They all had briefcases. Black, of course.

"Halloween coming early, Harry?"

"John ," Sandusky started his sentence with someone else's name, which, for him, was odd. His sentences usually started with the words *I, North Carolina Mutual Indemnity*, or *Harry Sandusky of North Carolina Mutual Indemnity*. "John," he repeated, "there's been concern about this missing armored car."

"So you've come for a surprise audit?"

"Well, you know, John , North Carolina Mutual Indemnity is a cautious company."

"With *three* auditors?"

"Oh, these gentlemen are not from North Carolina Mutual Indemnity. No, no, no. They are bank auditors from the State of North Carolina. North Carolina is concerned over this missing armored car. See, they," (pause) "and North Carolina Mutual Indemnity are concerned this . . . this . . . this matter might be a cover for a robbery. You know, while everyone is looking for the armored car, someone is making off with the cash."

Swensen shook his head. "Harry," and to the three men, "gentlemen, you are free to look over any of these records." He pointed to the bank of file cabinets along the wall of his office. "All you have to do is show me proper identification, and you can go to work. I don't know what you will find because these records are regularly audited by, I assume, your office."

There was a momentary pause and then Sandusky came back with an almost embarrassed wheezing. "It's not these records the State of North Carolina is interested in," he said. "It's the cash in the vault."

"Then what you are asking is a bit more difficult. The files," Swensen indicated the file cabinets, "I have written permission to show you. The cash is a bit more complicated. To audit the cash we have on hand means you will have to add up all of the individual 'cash on hand' accounts in those files," again pointing to the bank of file cabinets, "and then see whether the total amount of cash in the vault matches the number."

Harry started to say something, but Swensen stopped him. "That makes it sound easy. Unfortunately, it's not. As auditors are told every year—and keeping this as simple as possible for you, Harry, there are four different kinds of money accounts we keep separate. That is, when you walk into the vault, you will find four different areas where money, as in cash, is kept. One is for the federal government. The cash in that area are old bills going back to the Federal Reserve to be destroyed. As our bookkeepers take in cash, when we find old, torn, or faded bills, they put them aside. Once every six months we send them to the Federal Reserve. The *value* of those dollars is in the records of the individual companies so that none of the companies loses a dime. But the actual dollars are separate."

Sandusky started to say something, but Swensen waved him quiet again. "The largest part of our vault is for cash being held for banks. It's simply storage for the banks. The third storage area is for smaller businesses that need cash on an irregular basis. These businesses don't feel comfortable having, say, thirty thousand dollars in cash in the grocery store. So they have, say, fifty thousand dollars in storage here. When the business wants thirty thousand dollars, we send it thirty thousand dollars in cash. But . . . but . . . but . . ." Swensen held off Sandusky's question, "but the money is not listed in bundles by the business. It's just one big pile, so to speak, and we adjust the paperwork in the files." Again he pointed to the bank of file cabinets.

"The last area is where we keep privately owned valuables that includes cash. We have some packages deposited here, and we don't know what's in them. Some of our customers have packages with cash that we count and give them a receipt for the total amount, but we do not mix their money with any other money, and they are not part of our record-keeping system. That's because they may want cash on a moment's notice or are saving up to buy something for cash or for a reason they don't tell us. We don't care. Valuables in packages we leave alone. Money in packages that the client wants separate is counted, and they get a receipt. But we don't mix the money."

Sandusky nodded his head. "Thanks for the bit of education, John. The . . . our immediate concern is, all the money that should be in the vault *is in* the vault. The actual numbers can be double-checked later. There's just the concern as a result of the missing armored car, you know . . . you know . . . cash might have disappeared."

"It never has before, Harry," he said. "But," he looked at the three auditors, "I can see you have a concern. Show me the ID cards for the auditors, and I'll let them into the vault. But, Harry, you can't go in without a warrant. You're not a North Carolina auditor." As the men reached into their jackets, presumably for identification, Swensen continued. "But we have security procedures here as well. It is unusual for anyone to show up and want to count the cash. So, to be on the safe side, I'm going to have some Sandersonville police officers here. To be on the safe side. It'll take a while for some officers to get here, so, until then, please feel free to sit in the breakroom," he pointed toward a doorway in the back of his office, "until they get here."

Chapter 28

Captain Heinz Noonan, the "Bearded Holmes" of the Sandersonville Police Department, knew he was being played. He had an excellent sense of smell. But this was not the sense that detected the difference between pungent and putrid. It was the ability to detect the miasma of the approaching stench of politics long before the main cloud arrived. That smell was as fragrant as a breeze blowing over an outhouse.

Noonan divided the world into two categories: people of sweat and people of show. People of sweat do the work. People of show grab the glory. Noonan was a person of sweat. He worked alone because that is the way of the people of sweat. Yes, they often worked on teams but most often with other people of sweat. People of show were like circling vultures. They would arrive at the most propitious moment to take full credit for the results produced by the people of sweat. At that pivotal moment, the most dangerous square foot in America was between a person of show and a television camera.

Noonan had been ordered to examine money in a vault. Examine? What exactly did *examine* mean? A physician examines a patient because the physician knows what he is looking for. A biologist examines a specimen for what he or she expects to find. Noonan did not have the slightest idea what he was supposed to look for, much less what to do about what he found—if he knew what he was looking for in the first place. Then there was the reference to *sequestering*. You can sequester people, as in jury. You just move the sequestered people into a room by themselves. Or a hotel. But how do you sequester money? Money was, well, money. He could see sequestering counterfeit money as evidence in a trial, but he was not an expert on fake money. Exactly how was he going to know good money from bad?

Topping the fruitless cake was the poisonous frosting: these federal agents. The United States Department of Revenue, Financial Division, part of the FinCEN, Financial Crimes Enforcement Network in Revenue. Who? He was to be guided by these guys? The stench of politics was getting stronger.

Then the stink became overpowering. Noonan was to "use his charm" to get into a secure vault without a warrant to look at money he could not identify to report to some federal agents from an agency he had never heard of— (had Commissioner Lizzard checked to make sure there was such an agency and, Lord forbid, actually checked to make sure the men who said they were agents were, indeed, agents?)—to report what? Yes, I saw money, and it was there?

Jezz Louise and her brother Harold!

Then things got more complicated.

Noonan parked his Dodge Dart with 257,965 miles on the speedometer in the parking lot behind the Swensen Armored Car Company and was surprised to see four Sandersonville Police cruisers in the parking lot. It did not bode well when police cruisers were at the scene.

Yes, Noonan thought, it was going to be a fun-filled day here at the circus.

"You're late," the guard said as he looked over Noonan's identification. "Your buddies are already here and waiting for you."

"Waiting for me?" Just one more surprise for Noonan this morning.

"Said they were. The whole crew is in the president's office. They're waiting for you."

Dodging the mud puddles and oil patches, Noonan crossed the parking area, passed through the garage, and went down the hall to John Swensen's office.

As the guard had said, the office was packed. It was wall-to-wall blue. Police blue. Noonan recognized all the officers and spotted Harry Sandusky with three pipsqueaks in black suits who had to be accountants. (Who else dresses like that?) There were also the two

Cookie-Cutters from the federal government. The stench of politics was so thick here that Noonan needed a machete to clear the air.

The look on John Swensen's face was one of unrestrained relief. Noonan looked around the room and said, "What is this? Old Home Week?"

Before Swensen could respond, Sandusky cut into the momentary silence. "North Carolina Mutual Indemnity is pleased you are here, Captain Noonan."

"Really?" Noonan looked around the room. There was an awkward silence for a moment and then Swensen sliced through the cloud of politics.

"Well, Heinz, we have a situation here, and we need your assistance."

"Ooookkkk," said Noonan, stretching out the *O* and *K*. "I'm almost afraid to ask why."

Sandusky started to speak, but Swensen cut him off—again. "In a nutshell, Heinz, these three gentlemen," he said, pointing to the accountants, "are from the North Carolina Banking Regulation Department or Division or whatever. They want to examine the cash, the actual bills, we have in the vault. I have checked out their credentials, and they do represent the State of North Carolina. But I will not allow them into the vault without extra security. The money in the vault is not ours. It belongs to clients who store it here. So, technically, I am authorizing the state of North Carolina to look at other people's money. That makes me very nervous."

He paused and then continued. "What also makes me nervous," Swensen charged right over one of the Cookie-Cutters who was about to speak, cutting him off. "I'm running this operation, sir."

Looking back at Noonan, Swensen continued. "There is a problem with a client who has money stored here but is not in the audit system. What that means is the only record we have of the client's money are receipts we have co-signed with them. But as that money is in the vault, it's insured. The federal government, represented by these two gentlemen," he pointed at the Cookie-Cutters, "are from some alphabet soup agency in the Department of the Treasury. They want to know the money from one particular company is actually in the vault. They do not have a warrant to see the money, but I have no objection if a qualified someone verifies whether the money from the company is in the vault. That's where you come in. I need a neutral third party to look at the money in question and verify it is there. The North Carolina auditors cannot do it because the company in question is not under its jurisdiction. I will not allow the feds into the vault because they do not have a warrant. But if you, a responsible third party, were to examine the cash in question, it would satisfy the feds."

"So you want me to go into the vault with the North Carolina auditors and look at some money?"

"Basically, yes. You won't have to count all of it. You just must look at it and describe it to the feds. It will be on a palette in bundles of bills. You may want to take a few of the bundles of bills and thumb your way through to see if all the bills in the bundle are identical— one-hundred-dollar-bills in a bundle and fifty dollars in another. The feds don't need to know the exact amount; we have those records. They just want to make sure the said money is actually there. In the vault."

"OK," Noonan said, still trying to sort through why the mob of blue was there. "So all of us," he pointed to the men in blue, "are going into the vault at the same time?"

Swensen laughed. "No, not at all. You and the three auditors will be the only ones in the vault. These police officers," he swept the wall of blue with a wave of his hand, "are here for security. This is a very unusual situation, and since there will be people I do not know in the vault, I require some extra security."

"So do I," snapped Sandusky. Then he added, "That is, so does North Carolina Mutual Indemnity."

Noonan was silent for a moment. "The immediate question I have is, why. This is an unusual gathering, I grant you. But why are we doing this?"

"I'll take it from here," Sandusky cut in. "There's a missing armored. We don't know anything about the armored truck except it's missing. We," he pointed to himself and the auditors, "want to make sure while law enforcement is focused on finding the armored car, someone isn't snitching from the vault."

Noonan said nothing for a long moment. Finally, he said, "I am not here to second-guess law enforcement, banking auditors, or the armored-car company. I am here to help, so, yes, I will go into the vault and verify there is money as described. But I want to make it clear I am not responsible for any conclusions other than what I report. I don't want someone coming back in a week and saying I should have checked every package on the palette or I didn't know a counterfeit one-hundred-dollar bill when I saw it or anything else. I am just going into the vault to confirm there is a palette of money in paper form, and I opened, say, five or six packets at random and determined that the contents of those packets were bills in certain denominations."

"Speaking for FinCEN," one of the Cookie-Cutters said, "that's all that's required for us. Our office just wants confirmation the money is there. The amount can be determined through paperwork not in the vault. We just need visual confirmation the money, the cash, in paper form, is there."

Noonan looked at the auditors waiting for a response. When it finally became clear he was expecting a response, Noonan was given a lukewarm yeah.

"I want the 'yeah,' 'yes,' or 'absolutely' from all three of you. I am being asked to perform a very unusual task, one that law enforcement does not usually do. I am doing this at your request, let me make clear, and I do not want any hesitation on your part. You are basically asking me to confirm the obvious. So I want a good, solid yes from all three of you."

He got it.

But it was a reluctant yes.

"I guess that'll be the best I'm going to get."

There was not a scintilla of camaraderie in the room.

Noonan had been here before.

The men and women in blue were the people of sweat. They were the ones who had to do the heavy lifting. They were the ones who were going to stand around the armored-car garage like cigar store Indians while three midgets in black suits and yellow dogs were going to count money in bundles that have already been counted, recorded, reported, filed, and audited. It was a meaningless task, and Noonan knew exactly what was going to happen. The three auditors would do a Q&D, "Quick and Dirty," survey of the cash in the vault—which had already been counted, recorded, reported, filed, and audited—and wait for Noonan to do his own Q&D on the palette of cash.

This was all a cover so Noonan could get into the vault and see if the money that was *supposed* to be there, cash that had already been counted, recorded, reported but not filed and audited *was actually* there. It was an exercise in futility. Why? It did not take a genius to figure that out. The money was legal but had to be kept in cash form because it could not be filed and audited. Ergo it was marijuana money, the only legal illegal money in America. And Noonan was being whipsawed between the federal government agents and homeland security just to confirm that the money everyone *knew* was in the vault *was actually in* the vault—where it had to be because there was no other place else to store it securely.

This was Act One.

Noonan knew Act Two was coming fast.

He was right.

As the men and women in blue received their assignments, the Cookie-Cutters came over to Noonan. In a confidential tone he was told how *important* his assignment was, and he was the "eyes of the federal government" and that his confirmation was pivotal "in an ongoing investigation by the Department of the Treasury."

It was a crock.

Noonan knew it was a crock.

But he was in a political swamp to his knees.

"After I confirm the palette is in the vault, and there is money of an undermined amount on the palette, what are you two going to do?" Noonan asked.

"Well," said one of the Cookie-Cutters, "the Department," and he spoke the word *department* as it were holy, "has a variety of means at its disposal to deal with scofflaws and drug dealers. At the present time we are ordering the money held under this warrant." He picked up the warrant from the table. "The money is now under the control of the federal government. When it comes time for the money to come out of the vault, there will be an administrative hearing regarding its disposition."

"So this is drug money?" Noonan kept his face blank. He knew the money was drug money; it had to be. But he kept his tone flat. The Cookie-Cutter had made a mistake by mentioning "drug money." That was not a thing Noonan could do to fight politics, but he could twist the tiger's tail when he had the opportunity.

"We didn't say that," snapped the other Cookie-Cutter.

Cookie-Cutter one chimed in he didn't *say* it was drug money.

Noonan was about to say something when Cookie-Cutter two leaned forward in the tried-and-true-and-practiced motion designed to intimidate.

"There's a lot going on here way above your pay grade," he said menacingly. "There are national-security issues to be considered. Just do your job and let us do ours."

Noonan didn't let so much as a flicker of annoyance cross his face. He waited a moment and then said, "You know, whenever I take a bath, I have to be very careful how I handle my towel."

The Cookie-Cutters looked at him and kind of shook their head like cartoon characters on TV who were trying to clear their thoughts from an off-center statement. Noonan didn't stop talking. He just rambled on as if the Cookie-Cutters were listening to him with rapt attention.

"When I'm standing in the tub, I have to be careful I don't want to let the bottom of the towel touch the water. If I'm not careful, and the bottom of the towel touches the bathwater, the towel will suck up the bathwater pretty quickly. Suddenly I don't have a whole dry towel anymore, just the very top of the towel. Not enough to dry myself. Has that ever happened to you?"

The two Cookie-Cutters just looked at Noonan in amazement and then at each other. Finally, one of them said. "Was there a message in there?"

Then the other one said, "Is this some kind of Banacek old Polish proverb that makes no sense?"

"Who knows?" replied Noonan as he smiled. "It's been my experience, so it's easy to overplay your cards. Sometimes you shouldn't even be in the game."

This did not sit well with the Cookie-Cutters. Cookie-Cutter one lurched forward for a nose-to-nose conversation. "Listen, old man. We know what we're doing, and what we are doing is far more important than some empty, missing armored car. You've got your instructions. Now get with the program."

If he had expected Noonan to flinch, he was disappointed. Noonan just smiled. "Not a problem. You just remember the story of the towel."

"Yeah, yeah, yeah," said Cookie-Cutter two as he turned away.

Cookie-Cutter one followed, and before Noonan could move, John Swensen was advancing.

"When it rains, it pours," Swensen said. "As if your day could not get worse—"

Noonan did not let him finish. "Let me guess, it just did."

"Yup. Before you go into the vault, there are two people I am sure you are just dying to meet."

Chapter 29

Officially it was day off. Steigle didn't have scheduled days off. His definition of a day off was when he was not working. The security schedule was erratic. He might be told at noon he was working the next day or, more often, he would get a call between 10:00 p.m. and 7:00 a.m. telling him he was working and to be on deck by 9:00 a.m.

This was an odd week because the Jacksons were still missing. Which left the Swensen Armored Car Company down two drivers, so everyone had to do double duty. Steigle would be driving with no escort because Delgado and John Swensen were going to be driving another armored. Schanche would escort Delgado and John Swensen because there were pickups and deposits. Steigle was just doing pickups and returning them to the garage. No one was going to do check-in for the pickups because the check-in personnel were doing the RMD, LLC run to Ocracoke. John Swensen was going to be with the auditors and Sandusky.

Thus, there would be no duty today. The armored-car garage was crawling with cops, and the vault was going to be inspected. So it was a real day off.

Steigle's first stop was at the UPS boutique in Avon. He had put in an order for twenty large boxes. The flats were ready for him. Then he was off to the FedEx boutique in Frisco, where there were another twenty boxes waiting for him. By 10:00 a.m. he was at the rented warehouse garage in Nags Head. There was no security fence here, so he just drove up the garage door. After he was sure no prying eyes were around, he unlocked the garage door and rolled the metal plating up. Then he drove inside. Only after he closed the door behind him did he flick on the overhead lights.

Within an hour, the UPS and FedEx boxes were taped open and stacked in two piles against the back wall of the rented garage in Nags Head. Then he sat on the flimsy metal chair he'd picked up at a garage sale. He put his computer on the rickety card table from the Salvation Army thrift store and punched up the UPS on his computer. He printed out a dozen labels from the UPS account he had set up six months earlier. There was a single destination address for all the boxes. Then he did the same for the FedEx account he had set up nine months earlier—with the same destination address. Finally he folded ten *If it fits, it ships* boxes and printed out labels with a different address.

After he put his computer away, he made sure the box of vinyl gloves was on the card table along with several rolls of mailing tape. He double-checked the bathroom scales on the floor of the garage. His body weight matched on both.

Finally he checked to make sure the pickups he had bought in Vanceboro and Tarboro for cash started up. Both popped to life with no problem. He flicked on the headlights and did a walk-around to make sure the turn signals worked and no taillight was out.

You could never be too careful.

He turned the pickups off.

He hit the light switch before he rolled open the garage door.

The Swensen armored car was where it had been sitting since Saturday. Steigle was out of the garage and the door down in about ten seconds. He snapped the lock shut. It was pushing 1:00 p.m. Not bad for half a day's work.

Chapter 30

"Sorry to say it, Heinz, but this is your day for scut work." John Swensen waved Noonan toward the back door to his office. "It's one of those have-to-do-it meetings, and you should be there." Swensen paused as he indicated Noonan should enter the breakroom ahead of him. "It won't take long." He paused for an embarrassing moment. "Unfortunately, this will not be pleasant."

"Comes with the territory." Noonan smiled sadly as he entered the breakroom. "What great joy is coming my way?"

He didn't have to ask. As soon as he entered the room, he knew immediately just how much pleasure he was going to enjoy over the next half hour: none.

Gloria and Sandy, the Jackson wives, were as different as chalk and cheese. Gloria was statuesque with a perfect hourglass frame. She might have been all of thirty-five. She had blood-red lipstick and matching polish on her finger and toenails. She was wearing a tight-fitting top that accentuated her breasts and an immodest pair of shorts that showed off her long, tanned legs. Her high heels were open-toed and had a faux leopard strap over the top of her feet. Her makeup was perfect, and she had a bow in her hair. She was also smoking a scented cigarette in a cigarette holder.

Sandy was a hausfrau. There was no other way to describe her. She was a mousey, thin woman who wore what appeared to be a pants suit that was either a dull brown or a faded cordovan. She wore no makeup, and her hair was short, flat, and gray. She wore sneakers, and the last time her fingernails had been in a salon, Bill Clinton had been president of the United States. Her face and legs were ruddy as if they were sunburned.

But the moment they opened their mouths, they were as peas in a pod. Both were outspoken and rude as opposed to hysterical. Gloria may have been the extrovert when it came to fashion and looks, but she was second fiddle when it came to presence. Sandy took one look at Noonan and tore right into him.

"I take it you're the hired gun who's supposed to find my husband? What the blazes have you been doing for the past two days? I mean, if you're so darn good, you should have solved this . . . this missing armored car by now. There wasn't a dime in the armored, so where's my husband? What kind of BS are you pulling?"

John Swensen tried to cut in, but Sandy would have none of it. "Gloria and I have been on pins and needles for two days now." She looked at Swensen, pursed her lips, and did a poor rendition of his speech pattern. "Now don't say anything to anyone, Sandy. Everything is going to be all right. It's just going to take some time to sort this all out."

Swensen tried to cut it, but Sandy cut him off at the pass. "Don't you schuss me, John Swensen. I don't know what kind of malarkey you are trying to pull, but I am not pleased. Neither is Gloria." She pointed to Gloria, who was concentrating on looking delectable. "We've got two missing husbands, and the best you can tell us is to be *quiet*!"

Then she turned to Noonan. "And you . . . you . . . whatever it is you are. You a cop? If you're so darn good, where's my husband? It isn't like this is a murder and you're looking for a body. People do not up and vanish inside an armored car. What kind of a bozo are you?"

This time Swensen could get a word in edgewise. "Sandy, like I told you, more than once, we don't know what is going on. We've got a missing armored car. Charlie and Harry were driving the armored. They went into the Pamlico Tunnel and never came out."

Sandy grabbed Swensen's lapels and pulled him down until she was eye to eye with Swensen—and she was five feet six inches tall. "Don't give me goulash. There was an escort and all. An escort! A security escort! What the Sam Hill were the four men doing? I mean, really. Security? Charlie Schanche has PTSD so bad, he shakes when he's on the pills. And the two fruits, really? That's what you call quality? The only one with any talent is George, and he can't do the job of four men. So where's my husband and his nephew?"

Noonan was quick this time. He had been here before. It was time for the 3Ds: defuse, deflect, delay. It was very political, and it galled the detective he had to stoop to such a generic tactic.

"Cutting through the anger," he said, looking at Gloria more than Sandy, "which I can understand, I still need your help. I don't know your husbands, so anything you can tell me might speed up this process. Can you," he said, looking at Sandy, "cool down long enough for me to get some facts?"

"Better be quick," snapped Sandy. "I'm not in a cooling-down mood."

"I can understand," Noonan said softly. Then to Gloria he said, "Your husband is Charlie. Did he say anything odd to you before he left for work on Sunday?"

"Everything he says is odd, what's your name?"

"Just call me Heinz."

"Like the Ketchup?"

"It'll do. Heinz. Like the Ketchup."

"Heinz, Charlie is a little boy in a man's body. He doesn't talk about the news or what the president is doing. He's a go-to-work-and-come-home kind of guy. He talks strange things, I guess you'd say, but it's about wrestling, WWF, and the Super Bowl and who's been injured and how all of it's going to affect his fantasy football team. He's like a little boy. I don't mind. I don't care about what the president does. I just want a normal life, and until two days ago, I had one. Now I don't know what I've got. And for what? Charlie couldn't have stolen any money and run away with the neighbor's wife. There wasn't any money in the armored, and our neighbor doesn't have a wife."

"He didn't say anything odd or usual the day he disappeared?"

"Not a word. Just his usual cheery self. Nothing special. Just a 'Good-bye, babe. I'll see you this evening.' That was it."

"Did you take anything unusual with him?"

"Unusual!" This set her off. "Unusual?! He was a truck driver! Nothing unusual about any of his days. He left home to drive a truck! He didn't even take lunch! It was just 'Good-bye, babe,' and 'I'll see you in a few hours.'"

"How about you?" Heinz said, looking at Sandy.

"Sandy," she said because Noonan was clearly at a loss for her name to keep the conversational personal. "I'm Sandy. She's Gloria. We're both Jacksons, but we're only related through our husbands. They're kind of third cousins on one side and fifth cousins on the other, depending on how you want to do the genetics."

Noonan did not correct her use of the term *genetics*.

"Your husbands are distantly related," he said, pointing to the two women.

"Nothing distant about the old families here on the coast," Sandy snapped. "The Jacksons grew up as one big family. Not always a happy family but a big one. My husband, Harry, is my age—fifty-eight. Charlie is forty going on nineteen. Same family, same town, one big happy family with Charlie and Harry on the outer fringes."

"I see," said Noonan. "Both men just walked out the door as if nothing was wrong?"

"That's the size of it," snapped Sandy. "Now, I've got a question for you. Where are our husbands? This is crazy! There wasn't any money to steal. Armored cars do not just disappear into thin air. Someone's been lying to you, or you're lying to us!"

Sandy took a deep breath, and Swensen seized the opportunity to cut the conversation off. "Sandy. Gloria. Harry and Charlie have been working here for fifteen to twenty years. There has not been a speck of trouble from either of them. I can't say I know what happened to them. They aren't gone as in dead and gone, but they are missing. I don't have a clue as to what happened, and Heinz here," he pointed to Noonan, "is working hard to figure out what happened."

"Well, he sure isn't working hard enough." Sandy was livid. "Not anywhere near hard enough."

"I have never lied to you, Sandy. Or you, Gloria." Swensen pointed at the two women as he said their names. "What I told you Sunday is still true today. I do not know what happened. I do not know where your husbands are. I do not know what is going on. All I can do is tell you to wait. Just like I am doing. That's all I can say."

"Well, you'd better do better than that!" Sandy was flushed. "A lot better than that."

Things appeared to get out of hand, when Noonan cut in. "I do have a couple of more questions, if you don't mind. I can't tell you anything about your husbands, but the more I know, the better I can help you."

"OK." Gloria rolled her eyes and seemed resigned to answering a few questions.

"First," Noonan started. "Do either of your husbands do any rock climbing?"

The question took them both by surprise.

"Climbing?" Sandy looked at him strangely. "Harry thinks our bed should be on the floor with no legs."

Gloria kind of shook her head.

"I take that as a no," Noonan said.

"Charlie's athletic, if you know what I mean." She smiled sheepishly. "But he doesn't go climbing cliffs and mountains, if that's what you meant."

"Do your husbands swim?"

Gloria gave Noonan an odd look. "This is North Carolina on the coast. *Everyone* swims. Or knows how to. If you mean was he a competitive swimmer—Charlie, that is—nope. If he was, I never heard him talk about it. Sandy?"

"Same here. Yeah, Harry swam in the ocean. But we're talking about swimming from a boat to shore."

"Huh," said Noonan as he thought for a moment. "Neither men were very physical. I mean, athletic types."

"Harry was good at changing television channels," Sandy said. "For him that's exercise."

Noonan gave Gloria an "and you?" look.

"Nope. He was strong for his age, does weight lifting to keep in shape for the job. Loading the armoreds. But that's it."

Noonan pretended to look at a notebook. Then he said, "Did either man talk about foam?"

"Foam?" Sandy again gave Noonan a strange look. "You mean like foam in a couch?"

"Probably not," Noonan said. "Maybe foam like in froth or a fire extinguisher."

"N-n-nooo . . ." said Gloria. "Nothing I can think of."

"How about you?" Noonan looked at Sandy.

"Well, Harry wrapped packages and used those foam balls to put around Christmas gifts. It's all I can think of."

"Last question," Noonan said. "Do either of your husbands have a pilot's license?"

That took them by surprise. Sandy chirped up first. "Really, Heinz as in the Ketchup. This is North Carolina. Where would anyone fly to? Why get a license when it's cheaper to pay for a ticket and drink all the way to wherever?"

"So the answer is a no?"

"It is for Harry," Sandy said.

"Charlie didn't fly. Why do you ask?"

"Because neither of the men have been spotted since the armored car went missing. The troops had roadblocks at both ends of the Pamlico Tunnel. No bodies have been found, so your husbands are still alive. But if they were not spotted at the roadblocks, they might have been flown out of the area."

Sandy and Gloria looked at each other. There was a moment of silence and then Sandy said, "That's just crazy. You're saying some plane was there on the roadway, and Harry and Charlie got in and flew away?"

"Maybe not an airplane. A hang glider. They might have glided out."

The two women were silent for a moment. Then Sandy said. "I don't see that happening. That would mean jumping off into . . . well, you know, thin air. Harry wasn't that kind of a guy."

Gloria shook her head. "Naw. I don't think so. Even if they did, where were they gonna land? There's a lot of trees and underbrush out there. No place to land. Not safely, anyway. No, I don't see that happening."

"Well, they weren't in the tunnel, and they didn't get picked up at the roadblock. They didn't climb out—you said they were not rock climbers—and they didn't fly out. That doesn't leave much to consider."

"Crazy, crazy, crazy." Gloria shook her head as she spoke. "No. Charlie wasn't a pilot. Harry wasn't a pilot. Flying?" She gave kind of *pfssst* with her lips. "That's just plain crazy. Plain crazy."

"That may be," John Swensen said exhaustedly. "The good news is, their bodies have not shown up anywhere. It means they're still alive. Where, we don't know. The police have an APB out." He paused. "Do you know what that is?"

"All Points Bulletin," snapped Sandy. "I grew up on DRAGNET."

"Good. There's an APB out for your husbands. If they or anyone using their credit card, buys a ticket or tries to cash a check, we'll know within seconds. They can't stay hostages forever."

"Whoever's got 'em has been doing a good job so far." Gloria shook her head. "We haven't heard word from either of 'em."

Chapter 31

Alaskan humorist Warren Sitka's sage advice for husbands is not to waste three days arguing about something that will take you one hour to finish. Heinz Noonan took the suggestion to heart on Tuesday afternoon. Everyone up the administrative food chain wanted him in the vault. There was no reason to disappoint. Or, as Noonan would say properly, "There was no reason to disappoint *them*."

So he did not.

Disappoint.

Or waste his time arguing.

What happened inside the vault was exactly as he expected. It was SNAFU if you happened to be of Noonan's generation, a cluster if you were from Charlie Schanche's generation, or, if you were under thirty, a moronathon. SNAFU was the term coined during the World War II. Cleaned up for a commercial audience, it was the acronym for "Situation Normal: All Fouled Up." The implication is, no matter what is on the design board or how careful the planning, human beings will, well, be human, and, mixing authors, "the best-laid plans of mice and men often go astray."

The term cluster—usually followed by a f***—was a term from the Vietnam War and had nothing to do with sex. It originated from the early years of the war when the press in Vietnam was not allowed in the field. As a result, all information *from* the field was presented by colonels and lieutenant colonels, who had clusters on their lapels as a symbol of their rank *who were not in* the field. The information they provided was to press people *who were not allowed* in the field. Thus, every news story was "we won" and "they lost" which everyone knew was a crock, but it was the only news "from the front," so the press had to use it.

Of more recent vintage is the moronathon, usually, and pronounced "moron-a-thon." The meaning was clear. It is a collection of people doing stupid things for an extended period of time.

Two other expressions came to Noonan's mind as he schlepped through the pea soup of political stench on his way to the vault. The first was "been there, done that." This was more than an exercise in futility. He was being used as a stalking horse. The real story was, the feds, those Cookie-Cutter lookalikes from FinCEN, wanted concrete evidence that the money, the cash, in the vault under the name of RMD, LLC, the marijuana money, was actually in the vault. They knew there was "money" in the generic sense in the vault; they just wanted third-party corroboration that the RMD, LLC money was there.

That was step one.

Step two was a bit trickier. FinCEN could not *seize* the money from the Swensen Armored Car Company because an armored-car company was not a bank. Somehow FinCEN would have to convince a judge that the Swensen Armored Car Company was acting *as a bank*. This would be hard because banks are regulated by an alphabet soup of state and federal agencies, while armored-car companies are transportation businesses. They do not make loans. They do not pay interest on assets in their possession. They are not regulated by the FDIC, SEC, or, for that matter, state financial departments or divisions.

FinCEN could not legally seize the money because the money was legally acquired. But FinCEN could sequester it. Maybe. *Sequestering* the cash would do the same as *seizing* it. In either case, the money would be under federal control. Once sequestering happened, a collection of law-abiding businesses making money legally could be—and would be—shut down for political reasons.

The second expression that came to his mind as Noonan entered the vault was "same old, same old." FinCEN was playing the same old game. When you cannot win honestly, cheat.

Noonan's problem was tightly wound with FinCEN. Those Cookie-Cutter agents had played with Homeland Security Commissioner Lizzard like a fiddle. Lizzard was no dummy when it came to politics. He was not smart enough to know *why* he was being played, but he was astute enough to keep his fingers out of the frying pan. If Noonan did what he was told, Lizzard was going to claim credit for "breaking up a drug ring." If the entire affair fizzled, Noonan was going to take the heat for failing to "break up a drug ring."

But there was one thing Lizzard was not: a creative thinker. Neither, it was becoming evident, were the Cookie-Cutter agents. They were all charging down a well-worn path with no thought whatsoever of the possibility they were in error. This was actually in Noonan's favor: Blessed are they who are ignorant, for they are happy in thinking they know everything.

John Swensen could read the tea leaves as well. He opened the door to the vault and escorted the three State of North Carolina auditors into the secure room behind Noonan. Then Swensen closed the door behind them. He was not going to be a party to this charade.

"Well," said one of the auditors with a fake, tired look on his face. "The money you are supposed to verify is on the palette over there." He pointed to a lonely palette against the far wall of the vault. "You go do your counting, and we'll do ours."

But he and the other auditors made no effort to even bother to make it appear they were counting, tabulating, counting, computing, enumerating, auditing, checking, investigating, verifying, or balancing any accounts, books, receipts, cash, or records. The three men simply sat on three metal chairs in a circle and talked in hushed tones.

"Been there, done that," Noonan said to himself quietly as he surveyed the palette.

Noonan had seen money on palettes before, but this collection was a bit different. In the past, the money he had seen on palettes were clean and usually in bundles of one-hundred-dollar bills. That was not the case here. There were bundles of one-hundred-dollar bills, but there were also bundles of twenty-dollar, ten-dollar, five-dollar, and even one-dollar bills. Noonan knew it in an instant because the bill bundles facing up were of different denominations. When he picked up a random bundle and fanned through it, he saw all the same denomination of bills, but the cash had been folded, balled up, stained, or were greasy.

Noonan putzed around for about ten minutes trying to appear busy. FinCEN wanted him to look at random bundles, so he did. But he did not look very hard. Just hard enough the circle of auditors could say Noonan gave it the old college try. And that's what it was. In his mind, he quoted Babe Ruth—from his father's generation—who said the old college try "was playing to the grandstand or making strenuous effort to field a ball that obviously cannot be handled."

After he had spent enough time to make it appear he had given it the old college try, he twisted a concerned look on his face as he approached the auditors. "I'm gonna win an Academy Award for this," he silently said to himself. "Time to toss the dead rat in the punch bowl at the cotillion."

"Well," he said, wiping his brow, which had no sweat. "I've got good news, bad news, and no news. Which do you gentlemen want first?"

This took them by surprise. Auditors are not used to surprises. Mathematics is the queen of the sciences because everything adds up. Everything must add up. That's why it's called accounting. Every penny is accounted for. Numbers are never *missed*; they are just *misplaced* or debits hiding as credits (or vice versa). Accountants do not have an understanding of good news, bad news, or no news. They are human calculators with less personality than a computer.

"The good news is, I did look over the money—cash, I guess, you'd call it. It's there." He turned sideways and pointed to the palette. "The bad news is, I cannot tell you a thing about the money. I cannot tell you how much is there. I cannot tell you who owns it. I cannot tell you how it got here. The no news is, I guess there is about one thousand pounds of paper."

One of the accountants gave a sick smile and handed him a sheet of paper. "OK. All you have to do is sign this sheet, and we'll be through."

Noonan looked over the sheet and gave every indication he was reading the wording. Then he handed the sheet back to the accountant. "I can't sign this. I don't know this money belongs to this RMC, LLC." He tapped the document. "I don't know it amounts to ten million dollars, and I have no way of assuring a court," he shook the sheet, "there is an unbroken evidentiary chain of custody.

All I can say is I saw about one thousand pounds of American dollars, whose origin I cannot detect and whose ownership I have no documentation to prove."

This did not sit well with the auditors. They were not used to this kind of talk from law-enforcement people. But then, again, they did not deal with cops or money. They dealt with numbers, and numbers do not lie. Numbers do not necessarily tell the truth, but they do not lie. Accountants put black (or red) numbers on blank sheets of paper—actually in electronic columns—and then auditors look to see if the debits equal the credits.

Noonan's response took their breath away. Numbers don't lie! The money, the cash, was there! They could see it! Somebody owned it. So why wouldn't Noonan sign the manifest? They asked him that. Noonan said he would only sign his name to what he knew to be a fact, and there was not a fact concerning the 1,000 pounds of cash he knew for fact.

Things didn't get much better when Noonan and the auditors met with the Cookie-Cutters and Sandusky in the breakroom. John Swensen had the good sense to be needed in the garage. Noonan was on his own. But then, again, he was a master at steering clear of political disaster.

"The difficulty here is," Noonan said softly to the Cookie-Cutters, "you have a chain of custody problem. What you know will not stand up in court. I know; I've been there. To make a case, you have to show an unbroken paper trail of dollars and ownership. What you have now is a palette of cash with no proof as to who owns it. All the Swensen Armored Car Company knows is RMD, LLC is *storing* it in the vault. This does not mean RMD, LLC *owns* the cash. It is like a trucking company. A trucking company transports cargo but does not own the cargo. If law enforcement discovers drugs in a shipment in a truck, they do not arrest the truck driver. They go after the shipper. The same applies here."

Noonan tapped the sheet of paper he could not sign. "I can't verify any of this is true. Even a C-rated defense attorney would get this tossed before it ever went to trial."

"But we're not going to trial," Cookie-Cutter one whined as he broke in. "All we need to do is hold the money until such time as we can determine who owns it."

Noonan shook his head. "You will *never know* who owns it. Every judge knows that. No bank or business can determine where each twenty-dollar bill in the cash drawer came from. When it arrives, it falls into a pot. Like soup. When you add water to soup, it just thins the mixture. You cannot separate the water from the soup and say, 'This cup of water came from Sam and that one from Sylvester.'"

"But we need a third party to confirm the money is there," whined Cookie-Cutter two. "You don't have to say who owns the money."

Noonan had them. "This was whole point of looking at the money, wasn't it? You wanted someone to confirm the money on the palette was from RMD, LLC. I can confirm there is money on a palette. I have been told but do not know for myself the money belongs to RMD, LLC. Even then, just because the money belongs to RMD, LLC, the company could be a custodian of other people's or businesses' money. I don't know whose money it is; just that *you say* it's RMD, LLC's money. Besides, if you need a third-party confirmation," he pointed at the auditors, "these guys are better than me. They know more about money than I do. And they could see the palette from where they were sitting."

"Well . . ." Cookie-Cutter one started to crawfish. "It's not so simple. The RMC, LLC matter is federal." He pointed at the auditors. "They are from North Carolina. We can't cross our wires."

"You got that one right," said Noonan. "That's what you'd be doing with me. I investigate criminal activity. Technically there is no criminal activity here. There is no money missing, ergo there is no crime. The missing armored car is an interesting aside," he pointed at Sandusky, "but until North Carolina Mutual Indemnity informs the Sandersonville Police Department an item of value—the armored car—should be investigated, my hands are tied. You show me the crime, and I'll investigate. Right now, there is no crime. No one has claimed there is any money missing. No party has suffered damages I can tabulate."

"So you won't sign any sheet of paper as to the money?" Cookie-Cutter two was now pleading.

"I never said I would not witness or verify an alleged item that might—or might not—be pertinent to a legal investigation." Noonan was sensitive to lies—particularly when someone was saying he, Noonan, had said the lie. "I said I would sign a sheet of paper stating I had examined a palette of cash the bulk of which was in one-hundred-dollar and fifty-dollar bills, and I estimated the total amount to be about one thousand pounds, which is about ten million dollars. What I said I would *not do* was speculate on where the money came from or whose money it was. Homeland security specifically asked me to verify if a certain collection of money in cash form was in the vault. I have done so. I will sign an affidavit asserting I located some moneys *said* to be associated with RMD, LLC and estimated the value of the money."

"But such a statement will do us little good," whined Cookie-Cutter one again. "We need a chain of custody to sequester the money."

Noonan sighed; the cat was now out of the bag. Until this moment there had been no talk of why this money was important. But Noonan was no slouch. He had played this political game before. Too often. If the money had been illegal, as in mob money or gambling money, there would have been no problem getting a search warrant, and this little game of identifying money in a vault would have been meaningless. Not to mention a waste of time. This could only mean this money was marijuana money. The big money in the drugs like heroin, cocaine, and opioids was washed, particularly here on the East Coast. Money was collected into large amounts, like the money in the vault, and then flown to the Bahamas. A plane leaving Virginia Beach with cash for the Bahamas filed a flight plan for Orlando and then "got lost" on the way and ended up in the Bahamas. The Bahamians cared very little for what was coming in and didn't even bother to monitor many landing fields. The money was then trucked to a bank and put in a numbered account. Then the money was transferred to a bank in the Caymans or Europe and then, if needed, to a bank in the United States.

The money in the vault could not be money from heroin, cocaine, or opioids. Or mob money. Or gambling money. That only left one reasonable option: marijuana money. Marijuana money was legal in states where marijuana was legal. And marijuana money could legally be moved across a state line as long as it was not via the United States Post Office. The problem with marijuana money: it could not go through a bank.

Why this particular collection of money was in the vault was the real question. Under normal circumstances—or normally as Noonan saw it—marijuana money could go directly to the Bahamas and be deposited. The problem was not getting the money *to* the Bahamas; it was using money *from* the Bahamas in financial transactions in the United States. The feds viewed money from Bahamian banks as washed and seized it for investigation. What this meant to the marijuana industry was, its legally acquired money could not go through an American bank or to an American bank from a Bahamian bank.

Forcing the money to be kept in cash in the United States.

But not in an American bank.

So an armored-car company vault was the best option. The money would be safe, secure, and insured.

But it would have to stay in the vault, earning no interest and not legally available for investments like stocks, bonds, or certificates of deposit until the feds removed marijuana as a Schedule 1 drug.

But the feds were not going to remove marijuana from Schedule 1 and were aggressively going after the legal money in a quasi-illegal fashion. Like this ballet around RMD, LLC's money. Cookie-Cutter one's comment confirmed what Noonan suspected. This was a witch hunt. Every year there's a witch hunt. The key to surviving is not being this year's witch.

Noonan looked directly at Cookie-Cutter one. "Even with a chain of custody, you've got nothing. No judge is going to let you take money you cannot prove came from an illegal source. If you could prove it came from an illegal source, you would not have needed me to look at the palette."

"We don't want to *seize* the money," whined Cookie-Cutter two. "We just want to *sequester* it."

"I don't see how you can do that either." Noonan shook his head. "I've been there, done that. Unless you can show real cause, no judge is going to let you hold money you cannot state definitively came from an illegal source. Whoever owns this money—"

"RMD, LLC," interrupted Cookie-Cutter one.

"OK," said Noonan. "RMD, LLC apparently owns this money. Anyone with this kind of money can hire the best attorney in town. You will be in and out of court in the life of a mayfly."

"Not if the money is *sequestered*," cut in Cookie-Cutter two. "All we want to do is *hold* the money. We're just legally seizing it or the moment."

"You don't need me to do that. You guys usually just do it. You know the old saw, 'It's better to be forgiven than ask permission.'" Noonan handed the unsigned sheet to Cookie-Cutter two. "I can't sign this." Then he indicated the auditors and Sandusky, who had been silent the whole time, "They won't sign it, and North Carolina Mutual Indemnity doesn't have the standing to sign it. Neither does Swensen's Armored Car Company. You're stuck."

"Maybe not," said Cookie-Cutter one. "I'll sign it. My signature will hold it for a while until we can figure out what to do next. We'll see what happens when we get to court. FinCEN does know a few friendly judges."

"Goody for FinCEN," Noonan said, smiling as Cookie-Cutter one signed the document. "But I'd advise you to remember the towel story I told you. You could end up trying to dry yourself with a wet towel."

Sandusky looked at the Cookie-Cutters. "What's this towel thing?"

Cookie-Cutter two shook his head. "It's one of those Banacek old Polish proverbs that makes no sense. Let it be."

"Who's Banacek?" asked Sandusky.

"When you get to be my age," said Noonan, "you'll know."

Chapter 32

Joseph Richiamo got a call at 4:15 p m. He immediately made three calls on his disposable cell phone. The first was to Lenny Rusnak.

"We are at go," he said. "I need your people gone, out of town, anywhere they can establish an alibi. They are not to return until Friday at the earliest. Cell phones are to go ghost in an hour. Got it?"

There was a grunt at the other end of the line—in spite of the fact cell phones do not have lines. "We are all ready to go. It's clearly time to get going while the getting is good."

The phone went dead.

The next call was to Curtis Jackson. "I don't want to know where you are. I just want your people out of North Carolina now."

"They're already gone."

"Good. All cell phones are to be destroyed."

"Already been done. Mine is the last. It will be like the Hittites in ten minutes."

"Hittites?"

"It's an old expression. 'He was like the Hittites: history.'"

"Good enough for me."

The third call was one-sided. "Examination of the vault is complete. Nothing unexpected. Time to move. Destroy the cell phone."

Then his phone went dead.

Ten minutes later the other phone was dead in another form: in the Atlantic. Into the deep water off the St. Petersburg Pier. Now the recipient of the call was going to have the best meal he could find to celebrate his 3 percent of ten-million-dollar commission and a piece of LLC pie.

Chapter 33

Far to the north of Sandersonville, North Carolina—and substantially to the west—there is a chain of islands named the Aleutians. The islands extend 1,200 miles from the Alaskan mainland and stretch so far west, the last island is actually six degrees into the Eastern Hemisphere. This makes Alaska the farthest northern, eastern, and western state. The last island in the chain, Attu, was seized by the Japanese during World War II. It was the first time Americans had fought a foreign enemy on American soil since the War of 1812. The retaking of the island resulted in one of the highest casualty rate by American soldiers in the Pacific Theater. Fifteen thousand Americans and Canadians invaded Attu; 549 were killed, and 2,962 were wounded or suffered injuries from the cold. Of the 3,000 Japanese on the island where the United States invaded, only 29 survived.

The Aleutian Island chains is just as famous for its unpredictable weather patterns. This is primarily because the southern shores of the islands are warmed by the *Kuroshio*, the Japanese current. The northern shores of the islands are on the Bering Sea, notorious for icy weather every month of the year. To illustrate the climatic disparity between the two bodies of water, during the winter the Bering Sea has a solid mantle of ice from Alaska to Siberia that can be up to fifteen feet thick. To the south of the Aleutians, the waters are ice-free.

Considering the distance between the *Kuroshio* and the Bering Sea is between a dozen miles and zero feet, the mixing of the weather patterns creates the most unpredictable weather in the world. Worse, weather systems do not build; they arrive. Weather patterns also change so quickly, flying in the Aleutians is not only hazardous but also time warping. It is possible to land in False Pass in clear weather and then suddenly be socked in immediately for a week with a storm no one saw coming. Having to crab to the port to take off from Cold Bay and then, halfway down the landing strip, being forced to crab to starboard because there are fifty-mile-an-hour winds at 180 degrees dividing the runway is not unusual. As Alaskan humorist Warren Sitka says, "Every time I think about flying in the Aleutians, I don't."

The best description of the weather in the Aleutians is it *arrives*. It just *arrives*. You cannot see it coming. You cannot predict its pattern. You cannot expect it to snow just in winter, and rain falling on ice pack is not uncommon. No announcement; just an arrival.

At 3:00 p.m. Tuesday, the future arrived at the Swensen Armored Car Company garage. It did not come on little cat feet like Carl Sandburg fog. It came in like Operation Overlord. One moment the Germans on Normandy were looking at an empty ocean, and in the next there were landing craft from horizon to horizon as far as the eye could see along the coast.

With the two Jacksons AWOL, the rest of the security personnel were doing double-duty. Steigle had come in from a pickup-and-deposit run and had gone back out on the road. He had one more run of the day and was expected back by midnight. Delgado and John Swensen had been split up by necessity. Delgado was on his way to Tarboro with an insured load, and John Swensen was doing a deposit run to a half-dozen banks. Charlie Schanche was up to his elbows in the mechanical shop struggling with a recalcitrant drive shaft. Noonan, Sandusky, the three auditors, and the Cookie-Cutters were in the midst of their discussion about who was to sign the official document as to the ownership of the estimated $10 million on the palette in the vault when the future arrived.

"You're not going to believe this," John Swensen said when he came into the breakroom door, looking directly at Noonan. "I know you're not going to believe this, but it's true."

"OK," Noonan said. "I'll bite."

"The missing armored car. It's back."

"Back?" Noonan was not often taken by surprise. "I never saw this coming" was all he could say. "You sure?"

Sandusky, the auditors, and the Cookie-Cutters were flabbergasted.

"What do you mean 'back'?"

"Where's it been?"

"What about the drivers?"

"Are you sure?"

"How do you know?"

"Don't give me guff."

"N-n-n-nooooo!"

There was a maelstrom of expletives until Noonan held his hand to silence everyone. "What do you mean, *exactly*, by 'the armored car is back'?"

"It just arrived. I . . . we don't know how. All of a sudden we noticed the GPS for the missing armored car had popped on."

"Where is it?" Sandusky was almost beside himself with fiscal relief.

"You won't believe me."

"Try us," said Cookie-Cutter one. Cookie-Cutter two simply nodded like a dashboard figure.

"In the garage. Here in the garage. Against the mechanical shed wall. I thought it might be an error, so I did a quick count of the cars. We're back to sixteen armoreds. The missing armored just arrived."

"Someone had to have driven it in," Sandusky said. "I mean, it didn't just get here on its own."

"Oh, I know that," Swensen said, giving Sandusky a mild "I'm not an idiot" look. "I checked with the guard. Six armoreds have come in over the past four hours. Three have gone out. Everyone coming in is checked for identification if the guard doesn't know them. The guard said no one he didn't know came in."

"Well," Cookie-Cutter one scratched his head, "this clearly means one of your *trusted* employees must have driven it in."

"Not possible." Swensen held up a logbook. "This is our logbook. Every delivery every day is listed. Every driver is listed. Every driver is accounted for. What I think may have happened—and let me say *may* because I don't know for sure—is someone who is not with the company drove the armored car into the garage. Incoming vehicles are not checked. Then the unknown person simply walked off the premises. As long as the person in question was not carrying anything like a box or bag, the guard would not have stopped him on the way out. Or her."

"Well, there can't be many people here," Sandusky said. "The guard must have seen someone strange; someone who was not a regular."

Swensen gave him another of those are-you-kidding-me looks. "Harry, this place is crawling with people the guard doesn't know. There's you and the auditors," he said, pointing to the three men in black suits. "Then there's the feds," he pointed to the Cookie-Cutters, "Captain Noonan here, and a dozen cops in blue uniforms. They're in uniform, out of uniform, they've got shift changes. I don't know who they are by sight. The only place with any kind of secure entry is the vault! We'll look at the security tapes for the garage, but, at this moment, all we know, all I know, is that the missing armored truck is back."

"So we don't know who might have brought the armored car back?" Sandusky was still perplexed. "Well, at least that's one less worry for North Carolina Mutual Indemnity."

"I don't have a clue how the armored got here," said Swensen. "And I don't care. Armored cars cannot sue! I want my drivers back! Where are my drivers?"

"I can't answer that," Noonan said quickly. "But we'd better lock down the armored car."

"I already have." Swensen was edging toward upset. "I didn't know what to do, so I told two of your people," he looked directly at Noonan, "to guard the truck. I also pulled the security tapes for the garage for the day."

"The armored truck and the security tape will have to go to the police lab," Noonan said. "For the moment, we'll have to lock down the garage."

"I have! But it's like locking the barn door after the horse has been stolen. I don't know how long the armored car's been there! The only reason I know it is here is because the GPS popped on, and I happened to spot it."

"Is there any kind of time frame on the GPS monitor?"

"Only when the GPS in the vehicle is one. Then it's real time. It will tell me where my cars are. I have never cared where they have been. I just want to know where they are in real time."

"Well," Noonan said as he stood up. "As of right now this place is locked down. How many armored cars do you have on the road?"

"Four right now and two set to take off within the hour."

"Well, I'm afraid those two are going to have to wait until we search them. Once they get a clean bill of health, they can go." Noonan had slipped into his professional mode.

"Looking for what?" asked Swensen, now starting to boil. "They're going out empty!"

"I don't know," Noonan said. "It's procedure."

"This is a business, Captain . . . er . . . Heinz. I have a business to run. I can't stop my business. Can't you just search the armoreds and let them go?"

"That's not up to me, but I'll see what I can do. Now, for the four armoreds on the road. When are they due back?" Noonan pulled out his notepad.

"Well, there's Steigle, and he's not due back until midnight or later. Delgado is on his way to Tarboro, and I don't expect him back until tomorrow morning. My nephew, John, is doing deposits, and he should be finished by six and back here by seven. And I have a new man, Jerome Muhammed. He's meeting another armored car for an exchange in Durham."

"Muhammed?" Sandusky suddenly became nervous. "Is he a Muslim?"

"I don't know," snapped Swensen. "And I don't care. He's new, but he checked out."

"Well, what's in the armored car he's driving?" Sandusky was jumpy.

"Nothing. He's doing a pickup."

"Are you sure he's not carrying anything?" Sandusky's nervousness was growing.

"Yeah. I checked him out myself. He's new. The new drivers get extra checking."

"You are sure there's nothing in Muhammed's armored car?"

"Not until he gets to Durham. Then he's got an insured load."

Sandusky came alive. "Well, we've got to check that armored car! We'd better be monitoring him every mile of the way. When's he going to get to Durham?"

"Oh, I don't know," said Swensen slowly. "Midnight. Maybe. Depends on road conditions. Why not just have the Durham Police meet him at the transfer point?"

"I don't know," said Sandusky carefully. "What if he stops and drops off something before he gets there?"

"Drops off what?" snapped Swensen, now visibly angry. "There is nothing in the armored car! There will be nothing in the armored car until it gets to Durham! Then the load is insured. Besides, we're concentrating on the wrong thing. Where are my drivers? The Jacksons?"

"Well, you know," Cookie-Cutter one started. "Now we've got a Muslin involved, and that changes a lot of things."

"Like what?" Swensen leaned across the breakroom table toward Cookie-Cutter one. "There is nothing in common with a driver who might be a Muslim with two drivers who disappeared two days ago! I don't care if he's a Muslim. I want to know what happened to my drivers!"

There was no point in arguing the point, so Noonan didn't. Hate it as much as he did, he was going to have to use the tool of Satan: his cell phone. Within an hour, Swensen's Armored Car Company was in lockdown except for three police officers tracking the four armored cars on the GPS monitor. John Swensen was escorted to the Swensen Police Headquarters when he arrived back at the garage at 7:30 p.m. Ramon Delgado joined him at police headquarters around midnight, and Jerome Muhammed was put up for the night in Durham. (His armored car was still empty.)

That left Steigle the only one on the road. When the monitoring began at 3:30 p.m., Steigle was stopped. He remained in place for about half an hour and then was moving again. He made several stops, which matched bank locations indicated on the GPS monitor, and then returned to where he had been when the monitoring began. That was at about 6:30 p.m. He was at the location for about ten minutes, then he was off. This time he wandered off the main road and made momentary stops at six different locations.

A little before 10:00 p.m. the GPS suddenly went ghost.

After five minutes, the Sandersonville Police sent a squad car to the last-known location for the armored car, a grocery-store parking lot with a liquor store, pizza parlor, hair salon, and a United States Post Office substation. When no armored car was located, the police put out an APB for Steigle and the armored car.

WEDNESDAY

Chapter 34

It took until noon Wednesday for Muhammed, Delgado, and the young Swensen to make it back to the armored-car garage. None of them were happy campers. Surly would have been a better description. First, they had absolutely no idea why they had been detained. Second, no one at the police station in Sandersonville or Durham had told them anything of substance. None of them were under arrest, but all were considered "persons of interest," and it was made clear if they did not cooperate, they could darn well sit in a jail cell until they decided to do so.

There was no reason for any of the three to be uncooperative. The problem was not that *they had* something to hide. It was they *knew nothing*, and that in itself was a red flag for the police. Cops do not believe anyone, and anyone who claims to "know nothing," at the very least, has information of value but does not know it.

Yet.

Thus, it is the job of law enforcement to "help them" recall information the suspects had no way of knowing was valuable.

The problem the police had with Muhammed, Delgado, and young Swensen was, there was nothing missing. Each of them were clean as whistle when it came to their record. Each of them had left the Swensen Armored Car garage on time. Each of them had remained on schedule, proof being the GPS tracking. Each of them had made every stop they were assigned to make. Muhammed's armored was empty when he was picked up in Durham. His armored was supposed to be empty. Delgado's insured load was transferred to him in Tarboro. Young Swensen's route was charted on the monitor, and Wednesday morning the Sandersonville police retraced the route and double-checked every pickup and delivery. They got zip.

John Swensen did not return to the garage until late in the afternoon. Exhausted, he had spent the night at the Sandersonville police laboratory watching the forensic team swab the armored car inside and out and match every fingerprint to the national database. Every fingerprint inside the armored car—cab and secure room—matched that of the employees of the Swensen Armored Car Company. There were a few fingerprints on the outside that were not in the database, but they were so small it was assumed they were children's prints.

The police paid special attention to the GPS. The problem was no problem. There was no sign of tampering. But it had gone ghost and stayed silent for two days. And the armored car had not been in the garage for those two days.

So where had the armored car been for those two days?

And where were the Jacksons?

And why steal an armored car that had no money?

Then there was Steigle. Rather, then *there was not* Steigle. He and the armored car he had been driving had simply vaporized into the ether. This vanishing of the armored car, Noonan said with frustration, was getting to be routine. On the *usual* side, Noonan said to the four men in the breakroom, Steigle's armored truck had been carrying cash. Not much, John Swensen said, but enough for a fine two-week vacation.

At the most.

John Swensen spread the logbooks for the previous three days on the breakroom table, when he got a cell call. Swensen looked at the number and then said to Noonan, "I've got to take this. It's your department. They want me back at your station."

Noonan just nodded as Swensen left the room. Then Noonan looked at the drivers who were still there. Delgado reached across the table and picked up the logbooks. "Do you want me to translate the books?"

"No," said Noonan. "Maybe later but not right now. What I want now are some answers."

"Well, we've already told the police all we know," Muhammed said and yawned. "Which is nothing."

"Maybe you think it's nothing." Noonan smiled. "But there's a lot you know which is just knowledge to you but important to me. So let's start from the beginning and see what pops, OK?"

None of the three objected, so Noonan started. "Muhammed, how long have you worked here?"

"Six or eight months."

"Who have you worked with?"

"Well, everyone. We all get moved around a lot."

"I know. You've worked with these two?" Noonan pointed to Delgado and the young Swensen.

"Sure. A lot."

"When you worked with them, were you all on motorcycles?"

"No, sometimes I drove and sometimes I rode. Like I said, we switch around a lot."

"Were you ever the senior on those trips? I mean, did you do the check-in when you rode or drove with them?" Again, Noonan pointed at the two others.

Muhammed thought for a moment and then said cautiously, "I don't know where this is going but, no, not really. The senior person does the check-in. In the six or eight months, I've been here for a while, and I've only done the check-in one or two times. That was because the truck was empty."

"So you never checked an armored truck when it had money?"

"There's security, you know. When the truck is going to have money, there's a procedure. The money is checked out of the vault and put in the truck. Only the senior people can do that."

"How many senior people are we talking about?"

"A dozen, maybe. Some of them are vault people. They're bonded and whatever, so they just work in the vault."

"OK, how many people who are not full-time in the vault are authorized to load the trucks?"

"Six or seven. There's President Swensen, of course; George Steigle, but you know that already; the Jacksons, but they're missing; and maybe Charlie Schanche. The rest of them have nothing to do with this missing armored car matter."

"Why do you say *maybe* Schanche?"

"Well," Muhammed gave the other two a strained look, "Charlie is . . . well, kind of . . . you know . . . kind of burned out. He may be senior, but he doesn't do any check-ins. He just rides bikes. Never drives."

"OK. So when someone does a check-in, he gets the money from the vault and loads it into the armored car. Does he do it alone?"

"Not usually. There's the person inside the vault who gets the delivery. The senior person signs the log and puts the money in the armored. But that's not the only way it can happen. If you have access to the vault, you could just go and sign out the money."

"So some senior person could go, steal money, and leave and not be caught."

"Could, but it hasn't happened yet. There's a pretty tight rein on the money."

"But it could happen?"

"Sure. But it hasn't happened yet."

"OK, when you check out an empty armored, do you actually look inside?"

"Yes. If I do the check-out, yeah. It's procedure."

"But you only check on empty armoreds. Have you ever checked out an armored with something in the back?"

"On runs where I'm making a delivery, like with an insured load, yes. I check the package, whatever it happens to be, with the log-in information to make sure they match."

"But not with cash?"

"I supposed I could, but I haven't. When there's a cash run, a senior does the paperwork."

"Who actually signs the log-ins?" Noonan pointed toward the logs.

"The senior actually signs the log."

"When you are riding security, do you see the senior sign in the log?"

Muhammed chuckled. "No. I don't know if it's protocol or not, but when I ride security, I wait outside the garage. There's a lot of activity in there, and the bikes would just get in the way. I wait outside, and when the armored would come out, we'd go."

"So when you are riding security, you don't check to see if the armored has cargo?"

"If you mean money, no, we don't check the armored. That's the senior's job."

"Do you stop at the front gate?"

"No. We just leave."

"How about coming back in?"

"There's no reason to stop at the front gate when we come in. We just drive into the garage and unload."

"When you come in with a load—I mean, when you are riding security—do you drive your bikes into the garage?"

"No. We drive over to the mechanical shop. We check the bikes in, fill out any work orders for repair. Then we walk over to the time clock and punch out. Then we just walk out the front gate."

"You don't check the armored at all?"

"No. We ride security. That's it. When the truck makes it into the garage door, we're through."

Noonan looked at Delgado and the young Swensen. "Anything Muhammed said not accurate?"

Both men just shook their head.

"OK." Noonan looked at Delgado. "Have you ever done a check-in with money?"

"One or two. I was senior for the day, so, yeah, I did the check-in."

"How much money are we talking about?"

"No idea. The money was in bags. I signed for the bags and put them in the truck."

"You never looked in the bags?"

"No reason to. I was given a bag; I signed for the bag."

"Who gave you the bags?"

"It didn't happen often. I've gotten bags from President Swensen, two or three of the vault people, Steigle, and once from an auditor."

"An auditor?"

"Yeah, there are auditors in and out all the time."

"Why would an auditor give you a bag of money? It would mean he was in the vault."

"She. The auditor was a she. Actually, I know why I was given a bag of money. And it was a big box, not a bag. It was old money on its way to be destroyed. It happens once every six months or so. The money is put in boxes and sent to an office of the Federal Reserve. It's just a delivery."

"But you signed for every one of those times you got money from the vault?" Noonan pointed to the logbooks.

"Every time. It's protocol."

"Every withdrawal from the vault should be in here?"

"Every single one."

"How about you?" Noonan looked at the young Swensen. "Do you want to add anything?"

"The only thing I could add, and it's something which just happened, my name is now on the vault list. That is, to get into the vault and check out money."

"Really? When did that happen?"

"Two days ago. After the armored truck went missing. John . . . er . . . President Swensen has been through chemo, and he's stepping back from the business. I'm getting increased responsibilities, so he added my name to the log in personnel."

"Have you actually logged any deliveries out?"

"Not yet. I was just promoted, if that's what you want to call it, two days ago. Since then we've been up to our ears in deliveries with the Jacksons gone."

Noonan looked at the three. "Do any of you know where the GPS is located on the trucks?"

All three looked at each other and then back at Noonan. All shook their heads.

"So the GPS is not an electronics something you turn on when you leave the garage and then turn off when you get back?"

"I know all the trucks have GPS," Muhammed said. "But I don't know where the bug is located."

"How about you two?" Noonan looked at Delgado and the young Swensen.

Both men shook their head.

Noonan waited a long moment and then said, "A lot has happened since you've been on the road. Last night about 10:00 p.m., Steigle's armored truck went ghost. The GPS went off, and he could not be reached by radio or cell phone. Any idea where he is?"

This took the three young men by surprise.

"He's missing?"

"The GPS went off?"

"Was there money in the truck?"

"Steigle's not the crooked type."

"Has he called in?"

Noonan waved the men silent. "All we know now is Steigle checked in with a load at about three p.m. and took another load out. He was out the door on the second run and has not been seen since."

"Well, I don't know what to say," said a shocked Delgado.

"I don't what to say either." Muhammed shook his head. "Sounds like a robbery. I hope Steigle's OK?"

"There's more," Noonan said slowly. "About four p.m. yesterday, the missing armored showed up."

This also took them by surprise.

"Nnnnooooo way," said the young Swensen. "The missing armored? The one that disappeared in the Pamlico Tunnel? It just appeared?"

"Like black magic." Noonan made a poofing gesture with his right hand. "Poof, and it was here."

"How do we know it's the missing armored?" Delgado asked.

"The GPS for the missing truck suddenly came on. It was in the garage."

"In the garage?" Muhammed shook his head in disbelief. "As in, someone drove it in?"

"Yup," said Noonan.

There was a moment of silence. Then young Swensen said, "Someone drove the missing truck into the garage? Do we know who drove it into the garage?"

"No. But as you have said, trucks are not checked when they drive in. So whoever drove it in, just drove it in. Parked it in the garage and flicked on the GPS."

"Then just walked away?" Muhammed said.

"Appears to be the case," Noonan replied.

"Not possible." Delgado was now shaking his head. "There are not many of us around." He pointed to Muhammed and then young Swensen. "It has to be someone who works here."

"Not true." Noonan shook his head. "There have been all kinds of people in here since Sunday: police, auditors, insurance folk. They come and they go. Since no one checks the trucks coming in, whoever it was just drove the truck in and parked it."

"But there is a security tape," Delgado said.

"True," Noonan replied. "The police are looking at the tape, but so far they've got zip."

There was a long moment of silence and then young Swensen said suspiciously, "The only person missing now is Steigle. You don't think. . ." the sentence trailed off.

"That's exactly what I'm thinking," Noonan finished his sentence. "But right now it makes no sense. There's no reason for the missing truck to show up. If Steigle drove it in, why? Then Steigle drives another truck out? The other truck had money in it, but we're talking peanuts. If there was a robbery, the bandits didn't get much."

"And we don't know where the truck is?" Young Swensen shook his head in disbelief.

"GPS is off. So, no, we do not know where the armored is."

"Or Steigle." Muhammed mulled it more than said it.

"Or Steigle," said Noonan.

Again, there was a stunned moment of silence. Finally, young Swensen said, "This does not make any sense. The missing truck shows up in the garage. There is no way to knowing who drove it in. Steigle leaves in an armored with a few thousand dollars, maybe, and disappears. His GPS goes off. Seems obvious whoever is doing this knows how to turn off and on GPS. But other than that, there's no link. There is no robbery because no money is missing."

"So what is going on?" Delgado looked at Noonan questioningly.

"That, Mr. Delgado, is a very interesting question." There was a long moment of silence, then Noonan finally said, "The three of you can go for the moment. Don't leave town without telling me."

Chapter 35

There are many old platitudes that are just old. But they are not necessarily truthful. "A stitch in time saves nine," for example, is only true if what you are stitching is something of quality. You don't stitch a T-shirt valuing just four dollars and ninety-nine cents. It is not worth a stitch if what you are saving has little value. The veracity of this platitude has also changed over time. Illustrating with an historical aside, one of the keys to understanding American history before the Civil War is the verb "to fix."

In Colonial America, everything came from England, and it was expensive. The object itself was not the cause of the expense; it was the transportation cost. Something that was cheap in England was expensive in America simply because of the cost of transportation. As an example, if a merchant in London had a broken wagon wheel, he didn't bother to repair it. He simply threw it away. That was because it was cheaper to buy a new wagon wheel than repair the old one. Americans did not have this option. A new wheel was very expensive, so it was advisable "to fix" the old one rather than spend the money on a new one. Thus did the verb "to fix" become synonymous with what made America great: doing the best you can with what you have.

Other platitudes stress logic. "There is no I in team," but if you are a boxer, swimmer, track and field contestant, fine artist, or writer, you are *the team* and the entire team is *I*. "Good things come to those who wait" as long as stars are aligning, and you only "forgive and forget" until the next time those who you are supposed to forgive try to pull the same stunt again. (Fool me once, shame on you. Fool me twice, shame on me.) Money *can* buy happiness, and with great power comes great responsibility as long as you are not a spoiled brat.

The platitude that Noonan learned to be patently false Wednesday afternoon was "It is always darkest before dawn." Well, it was certainly dark. What Noonan had was a collection of disparate facts that were like loose pieces of a giant jigsaw puzzle, but they were all of different colors and textures. He could not be sure they were all part of the same puzzle. The only thing leading him to believe all pieces were parts of the same puzzle was because there were so few pieces. Worse, he had the nagging suspicion this case would be like no other. In most of the other impossible crimes he had solved, there came a light bulb moment where everything fit. When all the disparate pieces fell into place. He may not always have been able to prosecute the perpetrators, but he could solve the impossible crime.

This case, not so much. He had an empty armored car that had vanished and then reappeared. He had two drivers AWOL, and no bodies had been found and not a clue to their whereabouts. There was a senior security person who had gone ghost with another armored car that had very little cash, three auditors worried about a palette of cash they could not prove belonged to anyone specifically, along with the president of the armored-car company who was retiring because of cancer, dodging lawsuits by the wives of the missing drivers, and playing footsie with two federal agents who had no warrant for information they already had. It was a fine mess he had fallen into, to paraphrase Oliver Hardy.

Then things got worse.

It was pushing four when there was a knock on the breakroom door. Noonan looked up from the logbooks—all dozen of them—and said, "Come on in." The door opened, and in walked Chelsea Edison.

She did not look happy.

"Why the long face?" Noonan smiled. "I expected you to have answers because right now I need a lot of them."

"Well," she said reluctantly. "I've got answers to your questions, but you are not going to like any one of them."

"How do you know that?" Noonan was being funny.

It didn't last long.

"In what order do you want your answers: good, bad, or solid."

"Solid?"

"I only have one solid answer. It's about the foam. I've got goose egg."

"That's pretty solid. OK, let's just go through the answers slowly."

"It won't work if I proceed in that manner, but I'll give it a try. I checked with all gyms and places where you could work out from Hatteras to Rodanthe. Steigle and both Jacksons have gym membership. In Waves. Just far enough away from Sandersonville to be inconspicuous. How you guessed they had gym memberships I do not know, but they all do. The same gym, and they all pay their membership monthly dues in cash. All three have been regulars. I pulled up the check-in rosters, and they—all three of them—come in about the same time and stay two hours. I was able to talk to some of the attendants, and they know the three by sight. They don't always work together, but often enough they are considered a team. They do weights primarily."

"OK, hmmm . . ." Noonan said. "I expected Steigle to be a gym regular but not the other two. Go on."

"Of the seven names you gave me, all of them are current on automobile and motorcycle registration. None of them have a pilot's license. There are no liens on any of their properties—sort of."

"What is 'sort of'?" Noonan asked.

"It gets very complicated very fast," Edison said. "Let me finish with the solids before I answer that question, OK?"

"Works for me."

"All seven have cell phones, and the two Jackson phones are off. The rest of the phones are on and operational. Other than the Jacksons, none of the others have a business license or are in a LLC."

"The Jacksons are?"

"Another 'sort of.' Let me finish up with your other questions— and one of them is a lulu."

"I can hardly wait."

"Well, for my finish you'd better double strap your tutu."

"Lulu and tutu. That's quite an alliteration."

"I know what alliteration means, and it will be the only thing you know for sure for the answers I'm going to give you."

"OK. Go on."

"I could find no reference to foam in the background of any of the seven."

"Go on."

"Of the seven, only President Swensen, John Swensen, and Ramon Delgado vote. John and Ramon have signed a few petitions over the years, mostly environmentally and LGBT related. All three are regulator voters. President Swensen is a registered No Party, and the other two are Democrats. If it makes any difference."

"Probably not."

"Now things get convoluted."

"Hold on for a moment." Noonan dug through the pile of logbooks until he found his yellow dog. "Shoot."

"As I said, this will get very complicated very fast."

"I'm ready," Noonan said, pen in hand.

"First, with regard to the LLC, the Jacksons were hard to identify because there are so many Jacksons in the area. About five years ago, the Jackson clan and some scattered individuals put together limited liability corporations for land speculating. Basically, they were consolidating small pieces of property into large plots. The point was to be able to sell, say, twenty acres of land at one time to one buyer rather than having the buyer deal with twenty different landowners."

"Makes sense."

"Yes and no."

"I hate those kinds of answers."

"Yes, it made it easier to deal with one buyer, but no, not the way it was being done. What ended up happening was many people with small lots in every joint venture—" Before she could complete the sentence, Noonan finished it.

". . . and some people were only in one joint venture. Which made them very unhappy."

"Correct. So making a long land title story very short, the two Jacksons—and I double-checked to make sure I had the right ones, and I do because their wives' names are with them on the land titles— were part of a number of joint ventures until eighteen months ago. Then they bailed. Now they are not part of any joint venture."

"They sold their land?"

"Oh, if it were so simple. No, they still own the land, but it has passed through two corporate shells. They still own the land, but it's no longer listed as personal property; it's corporate property."

"So their names are not on any of the land titles?"

"Another yes and no. Yes, they still own it, but it is being held in trust to Curtis Jackson, a banker. And Curtis Jackson has the Power of Attorney for the land."

"So if the land sells, Curtis Jackson can sign, but the money goes—"

"Back through the corporate food chain, and the two Jacksons get their money."

Noonan chuckled. "Clever of them."

"Not really. The paperwork was handled by Inganno, Inc., a sole proprietor legal corporation in Vanceboro. See if you can guess who the sole proprietor is?"

"George Steigle."

"Oh, you are quick. Inganno, Inc. was established five years ago. There have been no complaints filed against it. It is listed as a general law firm. I found a few references to it on Google. Three of them were news stories where Steigle was quoted in support of his client's lawsuit, and one was a reference to his pro bono work for a statewide hospice."

"OK."

"Keep the hospice in mind for a few moments. It is going to come back like a bad penny."

"Go on."

"Going back to the LLC and joint venture, eighteen months ago, just after the Jacksons left the fray, there was a change in attitude among the landowners. For some reason, they stopped fighting each other and formed an umbrella group. The umbrella corporation— and it is now a corporation—Jackson Land—is represented by . . . by . . . by . . ." Edison let the sentence drag.

"George Steigle. This is getting easy."

"Bingo. Shortly after the Jackson Land was incorporated, it began negotiations with RMD, LLC out of Colorado Springs. RMD, LLC is also a sole proprietorship. The sole proprietor is a

Joseph Richiamo. I could find no links between Richiamo and North Carolina except for this land deal."

"Oh, there is one. We just haven't found it. How big is this land deal?"

"Adding up land values, in the range of ten million dollars."

"Not a small sum."

"For some reason the deal has stalled. Why, I do not know."

"So far everything is suspicious but above board."

"So far, yeah. Now things get goosey."

"I am waiting with bated breath."

"Remember you told me to check all of the names at the checkpoint set up by the state troopers outside the Pamlico Tunnel?"

"Yes, and?"

"I ran all the names through the DMV and got a hit. But it was an odd one."

"Do tell."

"The woman driving a heavy truck is dead."

"She died suddenly?"

"Uh . . . no. She died six months ago."

Noonan was silent for a moment. "The woman driving a truck who was stopped outside the Pamlico Tunnel three days ago was dead?"

"Yup. Dead six months."

"OK. Someone assumed her identity?"

"No, just her driver's license. There is no activity on any of her credit cards."

"How do you know she was dead?"

"It popped up on her DMV record. I double-checked the Social Security Death Index."

"Which means someone knew they were going to be hijacking the armored car, what, six months ago."

"Appears to be the case."

"Any clue who?"

"As a matter of fact, yes. I got the city of death and pulled up the death certificate. She died in a hospice."

And before she could finish, Noonan cut in. "Let me guess."

"You don't have to. You've already figured it out."

"Steigle."

"I could not get a solid link because of North Carolina rules on confidentiality. But Steigle is linked with the newspaper article. And now it gets spooky."

"All right. I'm prepared. Hit me with it."

"While I could not establish a solid link between Steigle and the hospice, the hospice is state-funded, so I could get a list of the patients. It serviced—their term—fifty-two patients over the past year. I ran every name through the DMV and got a hit, Jerry S. Sinclair. He died eleven months ago."

"And he has a driver's license?"

"Eleven months ago." She gave a long pause.

"OK, Edison, I know something is coming. What is it?"

"Jerry S. Sinclair also has a passport. And he used it. Jerry S. Sinclair flew out of Virginia Beach at ten p.m. last night. He landed in LaGuardia at midnight and took a two a.m. flight to London. He cleared Customs at Heathrow at eleven seventeen a. m. our time."

"So our bird is in the wind."

"If Steigle is Sinclair, yes. I won't know for a few days. Not until I get a copy of the photo on the passport. But I'm willing to put money on Steigle being Sinclair. We'll know for sure when we get the feds to give us copies of both passports."

"Any other surprises?"

"You have no idea what's coming. You said to see if any of the seven have passports."

"Yeah."

"Steigle and the two Jacksons do. The others do not."

"This is spooky?"

"No. But this is. The Jacksons are listed as being on board a cruise line which left Norfolk three days ago."

"They're on a cruise line now? This I was not expecting."

"I didn't say they were on the cruise line now. I said they were listed as boarding a cruise line."

"When did they board?"

"Saturday. The day before they disappeared in the armored car."

There was a long moment of silence as Noonan mulled this over. Finally, he said, "Just because they checked on board doesn't mean they were on board on Sunday."

"Maybe not. But they might be on board now. The cruise line left Norfolk and headed south. It's a five-day cruise to the Bahamas—round trip. If they left Norfolk on Saturday at five p.m., it puts them in Nassau at eleven thirty a.m. on day three, Monday. Then ship departed Nassau Monday at ten p.m. and arrived in Freeport on Tuesday at eight a.m. It left Freeport at three this afternoon and is now at sea. It's due to dock tomorrow, day five, in Norfolk at eight a.m. I contacted the cruise line, and they stated they could not verify the pair was on board. There are no set schedule for passengers, so they can eat anywhere at any time. They could confirm their rooms were used every night, but it's a verification that means nothing. If someone had a key to their stateroom, the person could have messed up the bed, thrown some towels onto the bathroom floor, and pulled toilet paper off a roll. It doesn't take much to make a room look used."

Noonan smiled. "Just to be on the safe side, we should have someone meet the cruise line when it docks in Norfolk. We should also get a passenger list to see if any familiar names pop up."

"I already have the passenger list, and there are no familiar names. All the passengers will have to go through Customs, and the FBI has agreed to hold the Jacksons until we can question them. Which means we'll have to go to Norfolk."

"No reason for anyone to go." Noonan smiled. "The Jacksons cannot be in two places at the same time. They were positively identified as the drivers, so they were not on the cruise liner. It's a red herring. I am sure they boarded the ship in Norfolk and checked their luggage. Then they just walked off the ship. Passengers are checked when they board, not when they go ashore. My guess: they checked in when they went on board and then just walked off the ship. There was no way for their re-board because they were driving the armored truck. Clearly they had a confederate on the ship go into their stateroom and make it looked lived in."

"But how are they going to get back on the ship so they can arrive in Norfolk with an alibi?"

"I doubt they're on the ship. I'm betting they took a plane to Freeport. If they landed at a small airport, all they had to do was flash their passports. They still have them. All they had to do to get on board the cruise line in Norfolk was show their passports, not give them up. They have their passports in hand. They pretended to board the cruise line on Saturday but came back here for the Sunday delivery run. They disappeared on the delivery run and then went into hiding for Sunday, Monday, and Tuesday."

"Why?"

"I don't know. I'm just guessing. They had to do something on Monday and Tuesday here in Sandersonville. Then they took a plane to Freeport. They're probably checked into a hotel in Freeport. They will say they liked the Bahamas so much they wanted to spend a few extra days there. That will be the excuse when they re-board the cruise liner and leave with their baggage."

"That makes no sense! The smart thing would be to re-board the cruise line at Freeport and come back to Norfolk. Then they can say, 'What missing armored car? We've been on the cruise line since Saturday.'"

"Because they had to do something in Freeport. They had to stay there a few days."

Edison's face indicated she didn't entirely agree with what Noonan had just said. "They can say they were on the cruise line since Saturday, but they were seen in the Swensen Armored Car garage on Sunday."

"Really? By whom? The only one who said he saw them was Steigle, and he's in the wind. The Jacksons have an airtight alibi. The only person who can prove them wrong is Steigle, and he's not around and not likely to come back any time soon."

"But they punched into the time clock?"

"Steigle could have done the punching in. He had access to the records and presumably the security camera. He was senior that day. He was senior *every* day. Right now the Jacksons are in the clear. No one here can definitively prove they were driving the armored truck on Sunday. I see Steigle setting it up that way."

"So the Jacksons are in Freeport?" Edison clearly did not want to believe it.

"If I had money, that's how I'd make my bet. They probably flew into a small airport, flashed their passports, and rented a room in a small hotel for a few days."

Edison nodded her head, but her face showed confusion. "But what am I missing? Why go to all the trouble of getting an alibi? And why is Steigle on the run? Where's the money? There was not a dime in the missing armored car. If the Jacksons are on the cruise line, what's the point? Where's the cash? What are they running from?"

"I don't know," Noonan said and then added, "Actually I've got a very good idea. It will just take some time to flesh out the answer."

Chapter 36

Chelsea Edison was barely out the door when John Swensen came barging in.

"Things are popping," he said excitedly. "We've found the armored car."

"You mean the one Steigle was in?

"Yeah, that one."

"Was Steigle with it?" Noonan asked with the innocent look of a child on his face.

"Thank God, no!" said Swensen, wiping his brow in mock relief. "If his body had been there, I'd be court for the rest of my life! He's got three ex-wives, and not one of them knows the meaning of fiscal restraint." He stalled for a moment. "Forget I said that. I'm concerned about Steigle. He's one of my longest-term employees. But we've got the armored car, and he's got to be close by."

"I wouldn't count on it," said Noonan dryly.

If Swensen caught the irony of the remark, he didn't show it.

Within half an hour, Noonan and a forensic team from the Sandersonville Police Department were on the scene.

But there was a problem.

No crime had been reported, so the police had to wait for a search warrant. It was close to 7:00 p.m. before anyone could get into the warehouse garage.

"How do you know this is where the armored truck is?" Noonan asked a police captain. "I thought the GPS for the truck had been turned off."

"You are correct, sir. We *assume* it's here. We backtracked the GPS to noon. The armored car came here directly from the Swensen garage. That was at about three p.m. It stayed here for a good hour and then went straight to the airport. It was there for an hour, until four twenty-seven p.m., and then it went back on what we have been told was the regular schedule. It made a few stops and then went ghost."

"You're beginning to talk like the armored-car people," Noonan told him. "But it doesn't tell me why you think the truck is here."

"Educated guess, sir. It was here for an hour. Why? We don't know."

"Well," Noonan pointed to a line of warehouse garages, "there are a lot of garages here. How do you know which one to get the search warrant for?"

"One of our people got a list of names of possibles. One was a hit."

"Who was the source?"

"Sgt. Chelsea Edison, sir. She's on her way here now."

"A quality lead from a quality person. What was the name on the warehouse rental agreement?"

"I'm not sure. It was a legal office."

"Inganno?"

"Could have been. I'm not sure. But it's a solid lead, sir. Whatever it was, it was good enough for a search warrant."

"That's justice for you. I need to go in first."

"Not without these, sir." The captain handed Noonan a pair of vinyl gloves. "This is reasonably a crime scene."

Noonan grunted and slipped on the gloves.

A patrolwoman snipped the lock on the warehouse entrance and raised the sliding door. Noonan was handed a flashlight as he stepped inside.

"Please don't—" the officer began to say, but Noonan cut him off and finished his sentence.

". . . touch the light switch. I know. Light switches have a lot of fingerprints. I'll let the forensic people turn the switch on. They usually use a key or piece of wire."

"Sorry, sir. I didn't know you were familiar with crime scenes."

"Not a problem. Nothing wrong with being doubly careful at a crime scene."

"Is this a crime scene?" The officer let the beam of his flashlight bounce around the empty warehouse garage and the armored car. "I don't see any blood."

"Right now we don't know what we've got. Ah," Noonan said as the overhead lights popped on, "let there be light!"

The garage itself was large, twice the size of a residential three-car garage. Unlike a residential car garage, it was not stacked to the celling with boxes, crates, fake Christmas trees, dog kennels, ladders, old filing cabinets, and garbage cans. This one was positively vacant. There was a rickety card table against the back wall with a rusted metal chair beside it. On the card table was an open box of vinyl gloves. There was a garbage bag frame next to the table, but it was empty.

Noonan spotted a pile of what looked like boxes and nudged them with his shoe.

"What are they?" Edison asked.

"You're sneaking up on me, Chelsea," Noonan said. "Come on in and take a look."

Edison came around Noonan and poked the pile of flat cardboard with her flashlight. "FedEx boxes. Hmm." She carefully lifted some of the flats. "And there are some UPS boxes too."

"I'll bet you find some *If it fits, it ships* United States Post Office boxes too."

"You are correct," she said as she kneeled on the ground. "How'd you know that?"

"It half answers your question of 'where's the money?' My bet? Steigle got money out of the vault. He could because he had access to the vault. While everyone was concentrating on the missing armored car that showed up unexpectedly, he was loading this armored car," Noonan pointed his flashlight toward the parked truck, "with cash. He drove the cash here and met the Jacksons."

"How do you know, or are you just guessing?" Edison asked.

"Just a guess." He pointed to the pile of flat boxes. "I'll bet they split up the money here. The Jacksons took their share of the cash and put them in FedEx and UPS boxes. The boxes were probably already labeled. There is enough room in this garage for two or three more cars. I'll bet there were vehicles in here ready to be used."

"OK, they put the cash in FedEx and UPS boxes. To send them where?"

"Freeport. The Bahamas. Which answers the question why the Jacksons are still in the Bahamas. FedEx and UPS will deliver anywhere. If I were a betting man, I'd say the Jacksons' share of the loot was sent cash in FedEx and UPS boxes to the hotel where they're staying in Freeport. As the boxes arrive, they are taking the cash to a bank and depositing the money. They can't leave Freeport until all of the boxes arrive."

"So the Jacksons put the money in FedEx and UPS boxes and then what? Went around and dropped them off in drop boxes?"

"Maybe. Probably. Most likely that's why they had to stay in North Carolina for a few days after the armored car went missing. They had to be here to divide the money. I'm guessing they didn't trust Steigle to do it for them."

"A good guess," Edison said. "If there is money missing from the Swensen vault."

"Time will tell."

"But what about Steigle's share?"

"My guess, he used United States Post Office *If it fits, it ships* boxes. He's on the move. I'll bet the minute he passed through English Customs, he was headed for the Continent. He could be tracked through the airport, but after he left the building, he'd be in the clear. He's holed up somewhere waiting for the boxes to arrive at some post-office box he set up months ago. The United States Post Office will deliver, just not always on time. Time was only critical to Steigle until he made it through Customs in England. Now, time is not critical to him. In fact, it's turned from a deficit to an asset. The longer he keeps his head low, we can't trace him. He might be in a *pension* on the Amalfi Coast or in a cheap hotel in Brindisi. Wherever he is, when his share arrives, he'll deposit the money in a numbered account in Switzerland. He'll pay his bills in cash. For seven years. Then he can do what he wants."

"Statute of limitations?"

"He's a lawyer and clearly a very good one. He knows what he's doing." Noonan pointed his flashlight at the card table. "Everyone used vinyl gloves, and there is no trash. Everyone showed up here to split the money. The Jacksons took theirs and did a tour of FedEx and UPS offices or drop boxes. Then they went to an airport and took a private plane to Freeport. I'll bet their wives are with them. I don't see those women letting their husbands have cash on a hot tropical island with no chaperon."

Edison chuckled. "That's a crude way of looking at it."

"Maybe. But probably true."

"For his part, I'm betting Steigle used the *If it fits, it ships*. All he had to do was go to any post office with an open lobby. He probably didn't need the automated postage machines. He could have paid the postage and downloaded the labels right here. I'm betting he visited several post-office lobbies just in case we figured out what he was doing. We might have been able to stop some packages—but not all of them. The Jacksons had to get the packages to a UPS or FedEx office before they closed. FedEx has some drop boxes, but they are in buildings that close at, say, six p.m. So the Jacksons had to scamper all over town to get their packages gone."

"But we can trace all the packages?"

"Why?" Noonan smiled. "Stop thinking like a cop. Pretend you are a clever criminal. Like Steigle. Let's just assume—and I'm not suggesting it's true—Steigle cleaned out the vault. That's a couple of tons of paper money, and there is no indication here," Noonan pointed around the garage, "that two tons of cash came through this room. The GPS on the armored car," he pointed to the truck in the garage John Swensen and two officers were processing, "recorded a stop here for about an hour. Steigle could not load two tons of money at the Swensen garage and then unload two tons here in an hour even with the help of the Jacksons."

"He might have been able to load that much if the Jacksons helped him at the Swensen garage." Edison smiled. "Which could have happened because the armored truck Steigle drove in was not checked on its way out of the armored-car garage."

"Good for you!" Noonan was ecstatic. "It's what I've been thinking. I think the missing armored truck was here the whole time. Earlier today Steigle drove the missing truck back to the Swensen garage with the Jacksons inside the back. When he got to the garage, the Jacksons slipped into another armored truck, the one Steigle was going to use on his scheduled run. Just before he left on the run, Steigle turned on the GPS in the missing truck. Then whatever organization there was, went south. The missing truck was hauled down to the police forensic yard along with John Swensen and the logbooks."

"But how did the Jacksons get whatever money there was out of the vault?"

"Steigle had access to the vault. Or, more likely, Steigle gave the Jacksons access to the vault."

"If true, there was a lot of paper to load."

"I don't think so. I think the Jacksons and Steigle only went after the RMD, LLC money. It was on a palette near the door. I figure it to be about one thousand pounds. Half a ton. At fifty pounds per trip, they could load the entire half ton in twenty trips, ten per man. Remember, you said the Jacksons had been working out with weights. Fifty pounds is not much for a man in shape. The distance from the vault to the back of the armored is less than a dozen feet. They could have taken half ton of cash in ten to fifteen minutes."

"Then Steigle simply drove out the front gate with the Jacksons in the back with the money!"

"The trucks aren't stopped on the way out. They just go. Steigle just went. He came directly here, and all three of them unloaded the money. I'm betting there wasn't a lot of trust, so they divvied up the cash right here. One thousand pounds divided by three is about three hundred fifty pounds per person. At, say, fifty pounds per package, it's only seven packages apiece. Then they scattered. I'm betting there were two trucks here. The Jackson wives showed up in a vehicle. One of the Jacksons and his wife took one of the vehicles from here." Noonan indicated the garage. "The other Jackson and his wife used the car the Jackson wives came in. The second vehicle here was for Steigle to make it to the airport after he hid the armored truck."

Edison smiled. "When you think like a crook, all things are possible. Let me see if I can put the rest of this together. The Jacksons had to use FedEx and UPS because those delivery services delivered quickly. The Jacksons had to be in Freeport, physically in Freeport, to get the packages. This meant they had to have already reserved the hotel room."

"My guess too," Noonan replied. "They had to have a place certain to receive the packages. They didn't have a mail box in Freeport, so they had to use FedEx and UPS."

"And," Edison was now beginning to like thinking like a criminal, "FedEx and UPS move fast. The delivery was going to be a matter of hours, not days. Once the Jacksons got the packages, they took the money to a bank. Even if we get a court order to see if packages were delivered to the Jacksons in Freeport—"

Noonan finished her thought. "We'll still have squat. All the Jacksons have to do is keep their mouths shut. We can't prove anything."

Edison shook her head. "Worse than that. If the Jacksons and the money are in the Bahamas, why should they come back at all?"

"If they're smart, they won't. Now Steigle had a different problem—two of them, actually. First, he had two names on two passports. He's not stupid. He knows we'll be on to him fairly quickly. He had to get out of the country as fast as possible and stay well below the radar. He would not be able to do that with FedEx and UPS shipments. We could trace him. Or at least know where he was. But there is no record of the packages he sent by the US Postal Service. Even moving at top speed, it will take the United States Postal Service weeks to identify the packages he sent—assuming Steigle only used one of the two names we already have. He may very well have a third or fourth name and have a third or fourth passport. Steigle had to use the United States Post Service because he did not want to have to be someplace specific where he could get the packages. He also needed to be able to mail packages after business hours, and the United States Post Office was his only option. He did not have to appear before, say, six p.m. All he had to do was drop the prepaid *If it fits, it ships* box into the deposit slot."

"So Steigle could be anywhere in the world."

"I doubt it. Anywhere in the European Union, yes. There are no more border checks. Once he left Heathrow, there was no way to track him. Even if we know where the three hundred pounds of American dollars went, he's long gone from there now."

"He's a clever boy. We may never catch him." Edison shook her head.

"That's not the half of it. You are correct he's a very clever boy. I'll make you a bet."

"Do I want to take this bet?" Edison was pleasantly suspicious.

"At this stage in your career, yeah. If you want to be a great cop, you must be a creative thinker. You must think forward. Don't just draw conclusions from what you see, anticipate. Using this case as an example, Steigle is a very clever man. He's been planning this heist for years. There are a lot of moving parts here, and right now we've just seen a few of them. As we get deeper into the crime, more twists and turns are going to appear. But there is one thing Steigle is counting on."

"Which is?"

"We are not going to go looking for him."

This took Edison by surprise. "I . . . I . . . I don't see that as possible. He robbed—"

Noonan cut her off. "Stop thinking like a cop. What do we have now? Do you know if any money is missing from Swensen's vault?"

"Well, no, but there has to be."

"There is only money missing when we're told by John Swensen money is missing. I think I know where Steigle and the Jacksons got the cash. But there is a very good chance no one is going to admit it is gone. It is going to be a quiet robbery; it happens, and no one admits it has happened."

"I've never heard of a quiet robbery."

"You will as you get deeper into your career. A lot of jewelry heists are quiet robberies. The thieves contact the insurance company and say they will sell the stolen jewels back at, say, fifteen percent. Then the insurance company pays the thieves and retrieves the stolen merchandise. It's cheaper for the insurance companies to pay fifteen percent to the thieves rather than one hundred percent to the insured. Then the insurance company pays for any damages, and everyone goes away happy."

"Is that legal?"

Noonan shrugged his shoulders. "If no one complains, there is no case. Legal is what a court of law says it is. If the case never makes it to court, who knows?"

"What does it have to do with this case, this quiet robbery?"

"I think I know what money Steigle and the Jacksons stole. Thinking like a crook, I'm betting that's all they stole."

"What? Why?"

"If they only stole from one source, the source I am thinking of, it will be a quiet robbery. It will be quietly settled, and the three will walk away clean. But if they took cash from another source, the other client might file a charge. Then it is a police matter. Steigle is too smart for that. He's not going to risk three million dollars by getting greedy for the, what, fifteen thousand dollars or twenty thousand dollars that was in that armored car." Noonan pointed to the armored truck where John Swensen was standing. "I'll bet all the money Steigle was supposed to pick up yesterday is still in the truck. Every penny of it. The only money that will be missing is from the one source in the vault."

"I find that hard to believe. We're talking about criminals here. They'll take your dime on the table."

"Stop thinking like a cop, Chelsea! Think like a criminal. And a very clever one like Steigle."

"You really think he's going to walk?"

Noonan shrugged his shoulders as John Swensen came over to Noonan and Edison.

"Strange," Swensen said to the pair when he arrived. "There are delivery sacks and packages in the truck. I won't be able to tell if anything is missing until I check the logbooks. Why would someone steal an armored truck *with money* and then leave the money?"

"That," said Noonan, giving Edison an I-told-you-so look, "is a very interesting question."

THURSDAY

Chapter 37

"You nuts-and-bolts people are a pain in the lumbar region, you know." Cookie-Cutter one was leaning against the door to the vault in the Swensen Armored Car Company warehouse. "Everything here is under control."

Noonan shook his head softly. "That's not what I was told yesterday. That was when you asked me to verify RMD, LLC had money here. Money as in cash."

"That was yesterday," snapped Cookie-Cutter two. "This is today."

Noonan looked sideways at Chelsie Edison with a I-told-you-so look. "That's not the point. The point is there is a very good chance money from RMD, LLC is missing. Gone. Stolen. I need to verify the money is still in the vault."

"Well," said Cookie-Cutter one—and it was a long, drawn-out *well*—followed by "that is not going to be possible. The vault is in lockdown until we get clearance from FinCEN."

Noonan pointed at the two men. "You are FinCEN! The same two who demanded I look over the cash *alleged to be* from RMD, LLC to verify it was here. Yesterday. You could not even get into the vault because you had a bad warrant. Now, today, you won't let me go into the vault and verify the money is there? The same money you wanted me to verify yesterday."

"Oh, you want to see if the money is there? Why didn't you say so? Sure, you can go in and check on the money. Except it's not there. It's been moved."

"Moved?" Edison cut in. "You can't move money from a vault that's been locked down. Do you have a warrant to move the money?"

"Who the Sam Hill are you?" snapped Cookie-Cutter two.

Those were the wrong words to say to a cop. Edison had no problem dealing with MCPs and knuckle-draggers. "Who am I?" She pointed to her badge. "I am the Pamlico City Police Department on loan to the Sandersonville Police Department. You are in Sandersonville, and this facility is in Sandersonville. I don't need a warrant for a look-see. All I have to do is assert I have probable cause to believe a crime has been committed. If you don't let me in to do a search, I will run your sorry a—"

Noonan cut her off. To the two Cookie-Cutters he said, "Look. There's no reason to get snippy about this. Officer Edison has every legal right to look in the vault. You don't even have a warrant to let you in the vault. Now, Office Edison wants *to see* the money. To verify it is there. But you are blocking her entrance into the vault. If you will not let her into the vault to verify the money is there, well, sadly, she can arrest you for hindering a legal search. How's that going to look on your résumé at FinCEN?"

There was a long moment of silence and then Cookie-Cutter two looked at Edison and said, "The money is not there. It has been moved."

"I know that," snapped Edison. "It's been moved to the Bahamas and Europe."

The statement took the Cookie-Cutters by surprise.

"That's . . . that's not true," Cookie-Cutter one finally said. "The money is in the possession of North Carolina Mutual Indemnity."

"So North Carolina Mutual Indemnity is involved with the theft as well?" That was a good shot across the bow, and Noonan smiled at the overreach.

Again, the Cookie-Cutters fell silent.

"Not exactly," one of the Cookie-Cutters said.

"Look," Noonan cut in again. "Let's make this as easy as possible. You say the money isn't here. Fine. Then you say it's in the possession of North Carolina Mutual Indemnity. Fine. We need proof the money still exists."

After a moment of silence, Cookie-Cutter one relented. "It's a bit more complicated than that."

"Not really," snapped Edison. "You, FinCEN, or North Carolina Mutual Indemnity or both either has the money or not. Which is it?"

"A bit of both," said Cookie-Cutter two reluctantly. "The actual cash, the money, has been relocated."

"For examination," said Cookie-Cutter one, quickly cutting in. "So there is nothing you can look at here."

"I find it hard to believe," Noonan said in a been-there-done-that tone. "And this is only the beginning of the problem. If the cash has been *relocated*, as you say, it is still the possession of RMD, LLC. RMD, LLC still owns the money. So, in this case, *relocating* is the same as *stealing*. You did not have a warrant to look at the money, much less relocate it. Now RMD, LLC has no money. No cash. That's called theft. Unless you have some paperwork to verify you—"

This time Cookie-Cutter one cut Noonan off. "Oh, RMD, LLC is not out of any money. No, no, no. You misunderstand us. FinCEN relocated the cash, the actual dollars. But RMD, LLC is not out a dime because the money is insured. FinCEN has the cash, and North Carolina Mutual Indemnity has been given the authority to issue an insurance check for the same amount. Yes, the cash is gone, but the value of the cash is in the possession of RMD, LLC. It's in the form of an insurance check from North Carolina Mutual Indemnity."

"So RMC, LLC has this check as we speak?" Edison was law-and-order suspicious.

Cookie-Cutter two tried to wade out of the rhetorical swamp he and Cookie-Cutter one had wandered into. "Look, people. We're all on the same side here. Checks take time. North Carolina Mutual Indemnity has agreed to cut RMD, LLC a check for the total amount of the . . . the *relocated* moneys. It's just going to take some time for the actual check, the physical piece of paper, to arrive."

Edison softened a bit. "Well, if that's the case, you won't object if I get North Carolina Mutual Indemnity on the phone and ask a representative of the company when the check will be coming." She paused for a moment. "I just want to make sure this banana has ears."

"Pardon?" Both Cookie-Cutters looked at Edison as if she were daft. "Bananas?"

"It's an expression my nephew, Jeremy, uses when he thinks something is unlikely. He says, 'Yeah, and bananas have ears.' It's now a family expression."

"Well," one of the Cookie-Cutters said. "In this case, the banana does have ears. Why don't you call North Carolina Mutual Indemnity right now?"

Edison did.

Harry Sandusky confirmed that a check in the amount "matching the certified deposit slips for RMD, LLC in the Swensen Armored Car Company vault" would be delivered within about thirty days.

Edison was not going to let anyone off the hook so easily. "What does 'about thirty days' mean?"

"Thirty days is thirty days, Officer." Sandusky's voice was as bland as his industry. "In thirty days the check will be delivered."

"To RMD, LLC?"

"Yes, Officer. To a Joseph Richiamo who is the legal representative of RMD, LLC."

"I see," Edison said. She paused for so long Sandusky had to ask if she was still there.

"Yes, I am still here. This is extremely important, Mr. Sandusky. I want to make sure I know, officially, that the money, the cash, which was in the Swensen Armored Car Company vault, the cash owned by RMD, LLC, has not been stolen."

"Oh no, no, no, Officer. Who told you that? Never mind. No, the money, cash, has not been stolen. It has been relocated. North Carolina Mutual Indemnity is cooperating with FinCEN and has issued, will issue, a check to RMD, LLC for the amount of the relocated money."

"What I am asking, officially," Edison pressed Sandusky, "is for you to say the money Captain Noonan saw the other day has not been stolen."

"Correct, it has not been stolen."

"Let me make sure I understand the situation perfectly. If there is an audit of the vault, there will be no RMD, LLC money missing. The money, as in the physical cash, has been relocated and is in the possession of FinCEN? And a check from North Carolina Mutual Indemnity for the same amount will be delivered to RMD, LLC. Is that correct?"

"Correct. A check in the amount of the relocated moneys will be delivered to RMD, LLC in thirty days."

Chelsea gave a "Well, that takes care of that" look, to which Cookie-Cutter one, quite relieved, said, "Happy?"

Chelsea gave a grunt that passed for an affirmative. She took a step to leave, but Noonan stopped her.

"One more thing," Noonan said as he held Chelsea by her forearm. "There are security tapes to monitor all the activity leading into the vault and in the vault itself. Will those tapes verify FinCEN actually took physical control of the dollars?"

There was a long moment of silence. The Cookie-Cutters looked at each other. Finally, Cookie-Cutter one said, "That tape is missing."

Chapter 38

Lenny Rusnak got the call well after midnight on his disposable cell phone, the number only the most important people in his life knew. He did not recognize the voice. He did not recognize the number. He did not recognize the area code either: 252.

"Yeah?" He tried not to sound sleepy.

"Lenny. Joe Richiamo. Just a quick call to let you know the First Sandersonville Bank of Trust is going to honor the incoming insurance check immediately."

"Joe, yeah, Joe. Sure. Say that again."

"Sorry to call so late, but I thought you'd like to know. The . . . uh . . . deposits you and your associates have been making has been relocated to a federal facility. In place of the cash, North Carolina Mutual Indemnity is issuing an insurance check."

"The feds took our money?!" Now Lenny was wide awake.

"That is incorrect," said Richiamo in a soft professional tone. "What the feds have done is allowed an insurance company to compensate RMD, LLC for the relocated money. The feds got the cash, and RMC, LLC will receive an insurance check. I am calling to let you know the First Sandersonville Bank of Trust is accepting the anticipated insurance check as a bona fide document. What this means is, the land deal you and your associates were anticipating will be consummated within the week."

"So we've wash . . . er . . . invested the money with no problem with the feds?"

"What I am saying," Richiamo was careful to enunciate because, after all, the telephone was a federally regulated entity, "is RMD, LLC is no longer in possession of the actual cash, your cash, which was stored in North Carolina. The federal government has relocated the money. To compensate for the relocation of the actual cash, the feds have arranged for North Carolina Mutual Indemnity to pay RMD, LLC a check in that amount."

"Our cash is gone?"

"Correct. Further, First Sandersonville Bank of Trust is accepting promise of the check. As RMD, LLC has indicated to you and your associates, the entire amount of the check—less my commission—will be invested in land purchases you and your associated have already approved."

"So we're getting the land with no hassle from the feds?" Now Lenny was ecstatic.

"There will be no problem with the feds because RMD, LLC is paying for the land with a third-party check." Richiamo then let silence fill the airwaves.

At last Rusnak was fully awake and got it. "I see. That's wonderful. I will be sure to tell my associates their legally acquired investment capital is now in the form of land in North Carolina."

"Within thirty days, sir, within thirty days."

"Well, this is . . . is wonderful."

"Have a good evening." Then the call went dead.

FRIDAY

Chapter 39

Friday morning Noonan put in a call to Chelsea Edison, Ramon Delgado, and John Swensen. He told all of them to meet him at the Pamlico Tunnel no later than 1:00 p.m. When he was asked why, he told them there were a few loose ends to tie up. One of them was how the armored car had disappeared in the Pamlico Tunnel.

That excited all of them.

He told them to bring a change of clothes. Old ones. They were going to get very wet. When he was asked to explain, Noonan just said to be at the tunnel by 1:00 p.m. And bring some towels.

Then Noonan hit the streets.

His first stop was at a hardware store where he bought several rolls of one hundred feet of heavy nylon rope, a pair of heavy work gloves, and a pair of hip waders. In the lumber department he had some plywood sheets cut into four foot by four foot sections. He also purchased a dozen brushes, plastic gloves, a plastic drop cloth, and a gallon of fluorescent yellow paint. He couldn't find a cheap pair of binoculars at the sporting goods store, so he settled for a spyglass at a hobby shop. His last stop was at the supermarket where he bought a five-gallon thermos, which he filled with coffee.

"Going to be long night?" The cash-register operator probably thought he was being funny.

Noonan didn't think so. "No. I just like coffee. This is my afternoon refill."

The clerk grunted and handed him his change.

It was a little after one o'clock when he made it to the tunnel. He was the last to arrive. "This is going to be fun," he told the three. "We are going to solve an impossible crime."

"But no crime has been committed," Edison reminded him.

184

"True, true," Noonan replied. "But in law enforcement you never want to leave a question unanswered. The last big one is how an armored truck can disappear in a tunnel."

"OK," said Delgado. "I'll ask. How?"

"I'm glad you asked," replied Noonan. "Let's see if we can figure it out together."

The young Swensen liked that. "Absolutely. I don't want to spend the rest of my life trying to figure out how an armored truck under guard can dematerialize in a tunnel."

Noonan smiled. "Come and help me unload some gear, and I'll show you whippersnappers how us old codgers go about solving riddles."

Delgado laughed, and all three began unpacking his car. Noonan spread the plastic tarp out beside the roadway and placed the gallon of fluorescent paint in the center. Then he laid out the four-by-four sheets of plywood along with the brushes and gloves. He had everyone put on vinyl gloves and set them painting both sides of all the plywood sheets. When they finished, they set the plywood sheets against a tree to dry.

"I hate to ask this, Captain," Swensen asked. "But what are you going to do with those plywood sheets? And why the fluorescent paint?"

Noonan chuckled. "Well, son, all in good time. You'll just have to wait and see." Noonan signaled for the three to come over to his car. Each was given a bundle of rope. He handed the spyglass to Edison. "Just put it in your pocket, Chelsea," he said as he put on the hip waders and the heavy pair of work gloves.

"You've got the strangest way of looking for an armored car," Edison said as she tucked the spyglass into her pistol belt. "Why didn't you get a pair of binoculars? At least they'd have a neck strap around them."

"Gotta watch every penny, Chelsea." Noonan smiled as he stood up and pulled the wader straps over his shoulders.

It was a strange procession entering the Pamlico Tunnel from the east side. Noonan, slogging along in hip waders, led the troupe into the tunnel. Behind him came Edison with the spyglass, and behind her came Delgado and Swensen gingerly holding the plywood sheets with the fluorescent yellow paint. The minute the procession entered the tunnel, they all flicked on their flashlights. Noonan had Delgado lead them to the alley where both men had found the scrapes on the wall. As Noonan was pointing out the scrapes, Edison remarked, "What do you expect to find here?"

"The armored car, of course," Noonan told her. "Now. Let's set the scene. When you two security guards went into the garage," he pointed at Delgado and Swensen, "you were not given any paperwork. It was just a routine assignment. You didn't check the truck to make sure it was a real armored truck, and there was no reason you should have. You two were outside in the yard, and the armored truck was in the garage. You assumed Steigle, the senior, was doing his job correctly. He was the one who did the checking, not you."

"Correct," said Swensen.

"When the armored truck came out of the garage, you didn't give it a good look-over."

Swensen thought for a moment and then said, "That's right. I just assumed it was an armored truck. Our armored truck. I guess I glanced at it and confirmed it was one of ours. That's it."

"That's what Steigle wanted. Earlier in the day he had taken the real armored car out of the garage. No one stopped him coming in early because he was known by the guard at the front gate. He drove the armored car out of the garage, and the guard at the front gate didn't stop him because the exit was routine. To keep his destination secret, he turned off the GPS in the truck—how it is done I do not know, but Steigle did—and he drove the truck out to the warehouse garage he had rented. The truck went in, and a fake one came out. It looked just enough like a real armored truck, it would be taken for real armored truck. I don't know where the fake truck came from. Possibly a junkyard. The point is, the truck was made to look like a Swensen Armored Car Company truck. But it was actually just a large pickup truck. The back of the truck was balsa wood. All of it. It was designed so it could come off easily at the right moment.

"Then Steigle drove the fake truck back to the garage. He wasn't stopped coming in because the truck looked authentic. Once the

186

truck was in the garage, the Jacksons got inside to drive it away. Steigle filled out the paperwork on the fake armored car just as if it were a real one. No one cared to check the truck because there was no money on board. When Stiegel came out of the garage, the two of you," Noonan pointed at Delgado and Swensen, "just gave the truck a glance. It looked like an armored truck, so, in your mind, it was. You started up your motorcycles and headed out. That was probably the last time you looked back."

"Correct," said Delgado. "I cannot remember looking back at all. But then, again, on the security runs I am not supposed to be looking back. I'm supposed to be looking for trouble ahead of the truck."

"That's how Steigle figured it. He knew all you'd give the truck was one quick glance across the parking area and that was going to be it. It looked like an armored truck. The vehicle was there, where it was supposed to be, and you left. You didn't know the truck you were escorting was actually a wooden frame set on a large truck. From the front it looked like an armored vehicle. The back of the armored was made out of balsa wood, which is why the trip to the tunnel was slower than usual. Steigle couldn't afford to let the wind rip off the back cover."

"This is a great story, Captain."

"Heinz."

"Right, Heinz. It's a great story, but there is not a shred of proof it happened. And if it did happen that way, what happened to the Jacksons and the woman who was driving the truck? Where did she come from? There was no one in the tunnel when we went through."

"That's right," agreed Delgado. "The tunnel was empty."

"The woman was already in the truck," replied Noonan. "She came in with Steigle. She was probably sitting in the back. All she had to do for whatever she was paid was drive the truck out of the tunnel. If she could make to a clean exit, all the better. If she was caught in a police blockade, all she had to be was Triple-C."

"Triple-C?" said Edison. "I've never heard that expression."

"Calm, Cool, and Collected," said Noonan. "It's an old law-enforcement adage. There was really no reason for the woman to worry. The fake driver's license was very good. It had her picture on it, and the license plates matched her name at DMV. Steigle had planned well."

"OK," said Delgado. "I'll buy the woman most likely was in the back of the truck. I don't see an alternative. But this still leaves the Jacksons. They didn't just disappear into thin air."

"In actual fact, Ramon. They did. We all know the truck went into the tunnel, right?"

There were mutterings of assent in the darkness. These were drowned by the noise of a convoy coming through the tunnel. Everyone waited until the convoy passed and the noise faded. Then Noonan continued.

"We know for a fact the armored truck came into the tunnel. The Jacksons followed protocol. Steigle and the Jacksons knew the armored car company wanted the escorted vehicle to be the last in the queue into a tunnel. If the truck must enter a tunnel being repaired—even if the truck is empty—the guards are required to take precautions. The entourage sends half the escort to one end of the tunnel and leaves the other half with the vehicle. Then the armored truck goes through unescorted. The security men on motorcycles couldn't see in the dark, so they'd be sitting ducks for anyone with a gun. That's how the company protects its people. The insurance will pay for any dollar losses, but you cannot replace a human life. The security guards also make sure the armored enters the tunnel as the last vehicle. That way they always know where it is, and if there is any trouble, no civilians get hit in a crossfire."

"And the Jacksons knew the escort had to place the armored car last. That was all part of Steigle's plan." Delgado shook his head in belated understanding.

"Right. The fake armored car entered the tunnel and stopped about here." Noonan flicked his light on the pavement. "Exactly here," he said as he flashed his light onto the walls of the alleyway, "there was some kind of a small, hand-operated crane. The minute the fake armored car arrived here, one of the Jacksons jumped out of the truck and attached a cable to the balsa wood super carriage. The super carriage probably was hinged so it could lift off as a single unit very quickly. All the Jacksons had to do was attach the cable in one or two spots and pull the cable. They'd probably practiced the move so much that they'd have had no trouble doing it in the tunnel in the dark. And while the Jacksons were pulling the balsa structure off the truck, the woman was replacing the armored-truck license plates with her own."

"Clever," said Edison. "Smooth and efficient. Then all she had to do was get into the truck and drive away. She only had to wait for the fake balsa wood structure to clear the back of the truck, the pickup bed. Then she caught up with the convoy and drove out of the tunnel as if nothing had happened. If the Jacksons were efficient, she could have changed the license plates and been gone in under a minute."

"Probably that fast," said Noonan. "I'm sure she practiced with the Jacksons. Time was of the essence, and they were making a lot of money for very little actual work."

"If this true," Swensen broke in, "what happened to the super carriage? And what happened to the crane?"

Noonan started to answer, but another convoy of vehicles drowned him out. When they had passed, he responded to the question. "Let's go find it," he said as he proceeded down the narrow alleyway. When he got to the junction of the alleyway and the hallway with the aqueduct, he stopped. But when he spoke now, he had to shout to be heard above the rush of water beneath the floor grates.

"The crane was temporary. As soon as the super carriage was pulled off, the men only had about four minutes to cover their tracks. The crane to be used to remove the superstructure was already in place, so there was time saved."

"Yeah, but *where* is the super carriage?" Delgado had to shout to be heard above the rushing water. "We searched this alleyway within ten minutes of the disappearance. We didn't find anything." Noonan heard the voice and recognized it, but the tunnel was so dark he could not see Delgado.

"You didn't find anything," Noonan shouted, "because you didn't know what you were looking for. You were looking for a truck. I'm betting the super carriage was hinged such that no piece would be wider than four feet in any direction. Why four feet? Because that's how wide this aqueduct here is." Noonan indicated the aqueduct below his feet. "It had been raining, so there was some water here. The Jacksons just pulled back the grate and broke the balsa into smaller pieces. They probably turned one of the grates over and crushed the balsa to splinters. The splinters went into the water and were carried out of the tunnel."

Noonan reached down and pulled one of the grates up. Then he stepped into the aqueduct. Water swirled to midcalf.

"Now, Ramon," Noonan's flashlight found Delgado and caught him in the beam, "I'm betting I find the crane and pulley in here. The balsa wood probably had water-soluble paint, so even if you found large chunks of it downstream," Noonan pointed in the direction the water in the aqueduct was surging, "the paint would have washed away, and you wouldn't be able to reconstruct the super carriage. But they couldn't toss the crane out. They had to hide it." Noonan's flashlight beam danced along the grates. "Get those grates up, and let's see what we can find."

Fighting the current, Noonan felt his way along the aqueduct. He covered twenty feet before he hit something. While the young Swensen and Delgado held one arm, Noonan reached into the swirling waters and pulled up a cable. Noonan pulled himself out the aqueduct, and all of them pulled on the cable, and out of the depths came a small crane with a hand crank. It was supported by two four-foot beams, each of which had a V-shaped head that could fit on corners.

Swensen examined the feet. "They would fit the marks on the wall, Heinz. You hit the bull's eye this time."

"Not yet; he didn't!" shouted Edison above the roar of the aqueduct. "What about the Jacksons? They never came out, and they couldn't stay here because this place was searched."

"Step this way!" Noonan yelled and sloshed his way down the hallway in the direction of the floodgate where the water exited the tunnel. At the end of the tunnel, the water rushed out of the aqueduct and arched skyward before it turned into a long, sickening, plunge two hundred feet down to the river below. By the time the jet of water from the aqueduct hit the river, it was a pelting rain that was gradually digging a hole in the river's edge.

"Pull these up," Noonan said as he indicated the last two grates of the aqueduct. "But first things first," Noonan said over his shoulder. "Chelsea, bring your spyglass up here."

When the last grate had been removed, Noonan ordered the four-by-four sheets of plywood be dumped into the rushing stream.

"Keep an eye on those plywood sheets!" Noonan yelled to Edison.

In the next instant, the four fluorescent-yellow plywood sheets jetted out of the aqueduct mouth. They hung midair for an instant and then plunged downward, twisting as air currents spun them. Two of them landed in the center of the pool and disappeared for an instant before bobbing to the surface. A third one landed directly on top of the first two and split into thirds, the pieces skittering across the pool. The fourth, finding a unique air current, landed closer to the shore. Here the water was shallow, and when the plywood sheet hit, it burst into splinters. Edison, watching from above through the spyglass, marveled at the show. "Quite a show, Heinz. Now I see why you wanted fluorescent paint. There's no missing it even from up here."

"Right," replied Noonan. "When we get down there," he pointed to the river below, "we have to scour the riverbank for whatever is left of the balsa wood super carriage; we can chart the river flow by where you find pieces of fluorescent wood."

Swensen pulled himself back into the hallway. "OK. So much for the super carriage. Now, how about the Jacksons. You say they jumped down there!" He pointed at the river far below.

"Not jumped. Rappelled. They had to leave from here." Noonan tapped the railing, keeping the four of them from tumbling into the river below. "They only had two choices. Up over the top of the tunnel and up the mountainside or down to the edge of the river. I'm betting they went down." He pointed down at the surging water. "Going up, they might have been spotted by a police helicopter. They had no way of knowing if one was available, so they couldn't afford to take a chance. Going down, they only had to make it into those trees running along with the river." Noonan pointed to the side of the river below.

"I'll bet if you look under this ledge running along here," Noonan tapped his foot on the narrow lip dividing the outside wall of the tunnel from sheer space, "you'll find some pitons, probably cemented in. They hooked up and dropped down right here. They doubled the rope so they could pull it free once they got down there," Noonan said, pointing at the water below. "Then they headed away from the end of the tunnel where the police were going to be stopping traffic."

Swensen gave Noonan a strange look and then looked at the rest of the troupe. It was clear no one wanted to go out onto the narrow ledge to check on Noonan's theory. When no one stepped forward, Noonan took up his own challenge. "Not a lot of brave souls, eh? OK. Give me about ten feet of slack and then tie it off to the wall. No, Ramon, I don't want anyone holding it. If I slip, I'm only going to fall ten feet. Then you can pull me back up. If you were holding it, there might be both of us making it all the way down to the river."

Delgado gave a sick smile and then gave Noonan about a dozen feet of slack.

"OK, now give me the end of one of those bundles of rope." Swensen handed him the end of a coil, and Noonan edged out onto the lip. He maneuvered himself awkwardly onto his belly and crawled along the ledge, his left hand gripping whatever outcropping or niche he could feel. With his other hand, he felt along the underside of the ledge. Inching his way along ten feet, he suddenly stopped. Then, with his left hand gripping the wall, he pulled the rope through what he thought felt like a piton. When the rope displayed firmness, he took a deep breath, and bracing himself with the taut rope on what he hoped was a cemented piton, he carefully pulled himself over the edge and looked underneath. As he suspected, there were two pitons spaced six feet apart. He was at the first. With great effort he pulled himself back onto the ledge and crawled back to the mouth of the aqueduct.

"You're shaking, Heinz," said Edison as Noonan finally stood erect.

"You're right, Chelsea," said Noonan with a sickly smile. "This is a young person's game." He handed Delgado the end of the rope that had been passed through the piton. "Now it's someone else's turn to white knuckle it. Somebody's got to go down and take a look around."

"Not me," said Delgado as he passed the rope to Swensen. "I get vertigo standing in front of the toilet." Swensen was hesitant; Edison was not.

"Men!" was all she said as she pulled the rope down over her head and shoulders. She wrapped the rope around her torso twice and then tied the end with a bowline. Then she stepped on the rope and pulled it tight under her boot.

"You've done this before," Delgado said with a smile.

"How'd you guess," she snickered and then walked over to the edge of the lip.

"When you get down, Chelsea, I want you to work your way up to the road. See if you can find anything showing two guys went through the area."

Edison nodded. She took one look down the sheer drop and smiled. "OK, guys, lever the rope through the piton and around the pillar. We want to be double safe for our colleagues in blue! It's time to rock and roll." When the rope was looped, she sat on the edge and dropped over.

"Now that's a gutsy gal," Noonan said as he looked over the edge and watched her recede down the sheer face of the mountainside.

After Edison made it down to the level of the river water, she unwrapped the rope from around her and pulled one strand of the doubled rope. The rope snaked free of the piton when she pulled it hand over hand. She left the rope on the side of the pool and maneuvered around some bushes and then waved excitedly back toward where Noonan and the other two were standing two hundred feet above her. She pointed in the direction of the roadway and began working her way through the brush on the steep side of the mountain.

"Well," said Noonan to the other two. "Now we know what happened to the dematerializing armored car."

"Guess that wraps everything up," said Swensen. "We've accounted for the money, the missing truck, and now the missing Jacksons."

"Almost everything," said Noonan. "Almost everything."

SATURDAY

Chapter 40

Noonan's arms were filled with a large cardboard box of Swensen Armored Car Company logbooks when he entered John Swensen's office on Saturday morning. Swensen was busy stacking correspondence in piles on his desk, so Noonan had to put the cardboard box on the floor by the door.

"I didn't get a chance to thank you for all the work you've done for us," Swensen said. "I can't pay you because you work for the police, but I'd like to give you something for your effort."

"Not a problem," Noonan said, smiling. "Protect and defend. It's our job."

"And thanks for bringing in the logbooks. John and Ramon are going to need them for the auditors. I'm not sure if you know it, but I'm more or less retiring from Swensen. I had a bout with cancer, and the good Lord told me it was time for me to step back."

"Actually, I did know, John . There is nothing pleasant about cancer. Active or in remission, it's like a beast in your bowels. It's always there, asleep. It can wake up at any time for any reason. It changes your life."

"Been there before, eh?"

"No, knock on wood." Noonan paused. "I just wanted to come by and clear up some last-minute items about this last week, you know, the dematerializing armored car."

"Quite an episode, I must say. Something mystery writers and conspiracy buffs would write about for years." Swensen put up his fingers in quote marks in the air, 'Vanished into thin air!'"

"That's what bothered me from the beginning," Noonan started. "I run on a two-tiered analysis on every one of my cases. Every aspect of every case has to pass that test. It's my way of double-checking myself."

"Interesting," Swensen said, half-listening. "A two-tiered test?"

"Yes," Noonan replied softly. "Every aspect of the case has to answer yes to the following two questions. First, is this action possible? Two, is this action reasonable? Take Bigfoot as an example. If someone tells me a Bigfoot was seen in the vicinity of a bank robbery, and must be the suspect, I log the accusation as *possible*—but not *reasonable*. For me to proceed down an investigative alley, the lead I am following has to be both possible and reasonable."

Now Swensen was awake. "Is this going somewhere?"

"Maybe." Noonan smiled and sat down on the upholstered chair in front of the desk. "When I was informed an armored car had vanished, I listed it as *possible* and *reasonable*. But when I was informed the armored truck was empty, that removed *reasonable* from the equation. It was not reasonable; therefore, there was something else going one, something in the background. In other words, something else was in play."

"Interesting," Swensen said. "Should I be taking notes?"

"Not really," Noonan said, smiling. "Since no crime has been committed, we're just talking."

If the statement calmed Swensen, there was no way to tell. "Go on," Swensen said. "I find this fascinating."

Noonan did. "A case like this—not that this is a criminal case because, as you know, no crime has been committed—is a matter of assessing degrees of subtlety. No one is going to tell you what is really happening. You will have to figure it out on your own. Fight through the Yaupon brush, as we say on the Outer Banks."

Swensen just smiled.

"Since I did not know what was going on, I went back to the basics. I followed the money. But, in this case, there was no money to follow. The dematerializing armored vehicle had no money. Ergo the money at risk was not in the truck, it was somewhere else. It did not take me long to pinpoint the RMD, LLC cash."

"But it was secure. It was in the vault." Swensen was slyly smiling now.

"Yes, it was in the vault. But there were minimal records. RMD, LLC basically had receipts. Those receipts just indicated how much money came into the vault. Your vault personnel counted the money to verify the amount, but that's all they did. What RMD, LLC was doing was similar to what the United States Post Office does. It puts mail addressed to you in a box it owns, whether it is a box in the local post office or your mailbox at the street corner. The post office only insures the delivery, not the value of the item being delivered. Swensen Armored Car Company was responsible for the storage of the cash from RMD, LLC, not the value of the cash. The Armored Car Company was not on the hook for the cash; North Carolina Mutual Indemnity was."

"True. But we, Swensen, pay for insurance. If we use insurance, we pay more."

"True, but only if you are on the hook. Which you are not. Neither is North Carolina Mutual Indemnity. The federal government is. And I must say the plot was admirably played. I am no slouch when it comes to subtlety, and it took me a while to put the pieces together. There were a lot of moving parts in this drama, and again, I must say, the mastermind played them well."

"Fascinating. And how did you figure out this fantasy of a crime that was never committed, if I can ask?"

"You can ask. You're the one who gave the answer early on. If you recall you said Swensen handled three kinds of valuables: audited moneys in the form of cash and debt-credit records, valuables along with insured items for transport, and cash being warehoused. The audited money was off the table because there were lots of people tracking that money. The valuable, insured items were being followed. Only one client was left: RMD, LLC and its cash, money. It was not being watched by auditors: private, state, or federal. But it was being watched by the feds." Noonan looked at the ceiling as he raised and spread his hands. "I wonder who tipped the feds there was marijuana money in the vault of the Swensen Armored Car Company."

"Whoever it was," Swensen said, with slight raising of one corner of his mouth, "there was nothing illegal, immoral, or fattening about it."

"Correct. The money was legal. If it had not been legal, the feds would have swooped down and snagged it right away. But that was the point. The mastermind needed the feds to know about the money but *kept from* legally seizing it. This forced the feds to do the only thing they could reasonably do. They got a third party, me," Noonan tapped his chest, "to confirm it was there."

"Hmmm . . ." was all Swensen said.

"And I performed admirably. I was played on a Stradivarius. The mastermind knew I could not and therefore would not confirm the RMD, LLC money in the vault was the property of RMD, LLC. All I could say was what I knew for sure: there was about one thousand pounds of cash on a palette in the vault that I *had been told*, but could not confirm, was the property of RMD, LLC. That didn't make the feds happy, but it made the mastermind ecstatic. A third party had confirmed the existence of about ten million dollars in cash in the Swensen vault that was not part of the regular audit scheduling. If it disappeared, Swensen did not have to answer to any auditors— private, state, or federal—but only to the insurance company."

"This is getting interesting," Swensen said. "But just one thing: if the money had been stolen, which it has not been, Swensen would still be on the hook, to use your term."

"Such was the beauty of the entire operation. The key to success was to stick someone else with the loss. The way to do that was have someone else take control of the money. But control had to be on paper and not on the cash itself. The cash had to remain in the vault, but the responsibility—on paper—had to be on someone else's shoulders. Those FinCEN agents never knew what hit 'em. They were not worldly. They seized the responsibility for the cash but not the possession of the cash. Brilliant!"

"If someone were planning on stealing the money, I suppose." Swensen was now openly smiling.

"Once FinCEN took control of the money *on paper*, the second phase of the operation went into effect. And I must credit the mastermind with his—or her—genius. The Sandersonville Police, the logical law-enforcement agency, who might have thrown a monkey wrench into the game, was busy looking for a dematerializing armored truck that never existed. The FinCEN agents were filing paperwork with their department, which left the mastermind free to complete the operation."

"Interesting. You said the dematerializing armored truck never existed. It had to exist because it reappeared."

"Ah, the genius of the entire operation. It wasn't done with smoke and mirrors but with a combination of high-tech and low-tech ingenuity. Everyone believes the GPS tracking system is high-tech primarily because it takes a high-tech system to monitor the movement of the GPS. In an operation like Swensen's, there are more than twenty vehicles. I bet they all have GPS. I'm also willing to bet no one is tracking the individual vehicles in real time. The system is just kind of on. There is no reason to monitor the vehicles in real time. If there is suddenly a problem, yeah, there will be real-time monitoring. But, for the most part, the system is like a light switch. When you need light, you use the switch to turn the light on. When you don't need light, the switch stays off."

"But the GPS on the dematerializing armored truck went ghost!"

"It went ghost in the garage. The GPS itself is just an electronic device. You unplug it, it goes off. I'm speculating because I cannot prove it; Steigle took the alleged dematerializing armored truck out of the garage on Saturday, the day before the truck went missing. The GPS was disabled in the garage, so the last-known location of the vehicle was there. Where it was supposed to be. Then he drove the armored truck to the warehouse garage where we found the other missing armored car. Sunday morning, he drove the fake armored car to Swensen's, right here, where the Jacksons were waiting. They immediately got into the fake armored car. It was Sunday; there was no cash to deposit into the truck, so the only person doing the checking was Steigle. Off the truck went. John and Ramon didn't give the fake truck so much as a glance. They were looking forward."

"Well, what about Charlie Schanche? He was behind the armored truck. Wouldn't he have seen the fake armored car?"

"He did because he was in on the deal."

"Well, if he was in on the deal, where is the money he was supposed to get for being in on the deal? The Jacksons are gone, and who knows where Steigle is."

"My bet—and of course I don't know for sure because, as I keep saying, no crime has been committed—is that Charlie got a piece of this business. He is probably very happy here in Sandersonville and didn't want to have to run. You're getting out of the business. Maybe he got a piece of the pie as you are leaving."

"Odd you should mention that." Swensen smiled. "Part of the reorganization involves Charlie. Because of its complexity, we are severing the mechanical shop from the armored-car operation. Charlie will own that operation and provide mechanical services to the new Swensen's."

"Amazing and quite a reasonable business decision."

"We at the new Swensen's agree with you."

"I thought you would feel that way."

"Go on. This is a fascinating fantasy story."

"I guess the Jacksons kept practicing the removal and destruction of the balsa apparatus on the dematerializing armored truck until they could do it in just a few minutes. At the same time, Steigle, who was providing pro bono services to hospice patients, was snagging identifications. We don't know how many identifications he took, but we know he snagged at least two fake accounts. One was the name he used for his passport, and the other was for the woman who drove the fake truck out of the Pamlico Tunnel. The fake armored truck went into the tunnel, the last in the line of the convoy. When the truck came to the alley, it stopped. The Jacksons levered the false back off the truck, and the woman with the fake identification switched license plates and took off. While John and Ramon were trying to figure out what happened to the armored truck, the Jacksons were destroying the balsa back and hiding the winch in the storm drain. Then they went over the side at the back of the alley and down to the river below on ropes. By the time the state troopers were called, the Jacksons were long gone. The identification of the woman—as yet unknown and will probably never be known—held up as did the license for the truck. The roadblock came up, and the woman and the fake truck disappeared, neither to ever be seen again."

"What about the Jacksons? Why didn't they just leave Sandersonville?"

"They couldn't. The RMD, LLC money had not been stolen yet. I'm betting they didn't trust Steigle. There was going to be ten million dollars showing up in the warehouse garage, and for that kind of money, no one is to be trusted. Besides, it was going to take at least three people to package the money quickly. I'm even willing to bet the two Jackson wives were there as well. Five people packing can go faster than three."

"Assuming what you are saying is true, which is speculative, how did the RMC, LLC money get to the warehouse garage?"

"Easy. The same way the dematerializing armored truck got to the garage. Steigle drove it. Steigle went to the garage and drove the supposedly missing armored truck back to Swensen. He didn't have to check in; he just drove it in. But the truck was not empty. The Jacksons were in the back. He parked the truck in the garage as far away from the vault entrance as he could. The Jacksons scurried over to the armored truck that Steigle was going to be taking out in an hour or so. Steigle then plugged in the GPS from the supposedly missing armored truck. It was spotted on the monitor or," Noonan let the sentence play out and then, after a long pause, added, "or you spotted the reappearance of the missing truck after Steigle had left. After all, you were the one who notified me."

"Oh, I can't remember details like that," Swensen said with a smile.

"Maybe not. But once the missing armored car appeared, everyone went over to see it. Including the vault personnel who, at that time, were a staff of two: you who were over with the reappearing truck and Steigle. Steigle probably opened the vault door, and the Jacksons went in and took out the RMD, LLC cash. There was one thousand pounds of cash, twenty trips of about fifty pounds apiece. The Jacksons had been weightlifting for a year by then, so fifty pounds wasn't much of a load. While everyone else, including me and the Sandersonville police, were ogling the now-reappeared truck, Stiegel with the Jacksons drove right out the front gate. Steigle drove directly to the warehouse garage where the money was put in UPS, FedEx, and United States Post Office *If it fits, it ships* boxes. It's a good bet the Jackson wives were there as well. When they finished packing the boxes, the Jacksons and their wives scattered to drop off the boxes in UPS and FedEx offices. All those boxes were for delivery to a hotel in Freeport, where the Jacksons would be staying. I'll bet you'll find the Jackson vehicles at an airport where they took a private flight to the Bahamas. The Jackson men were already on an APB alert, so they had to fly out on a private plane."

"So Steigle used the United States Post Office boxes. Why not UPS and FedEx?"

"To get the UPS and FedEx shipments, you have to be physically available. So the Jacksons had to be in the hotel in Freeport to get the packages. That's why they had to fly to the Bahamas. Steigle wanted to disappear. With the money. The best way for him to disappear with the money was to mail it to himself at some address where he did not have to be physically present when it arrived. Maybe a *pension* where records are not kept for short-term residents. He arrives at the *pension*, has a note from the post office to pick up a package. Picks up the package and puts the money in a bank or a safety-deposit box in Europe. Most likely Switzerland, a land where bankers ask no questions. Steigle might have flown out of the Untitled States on a fake passport, but at this point, as there is no crime, Steigle can go back to his own name. But his bank account, if in Switzerland, is numbered, so his name is immaterial."

"This is all fine and good, Heinz, but there are some questions remaining. If the ten million dollars really was stolen, then RMD, LLC is out of the money. It doesn't have the money. The feds don't have the money. And Swensen sure doesn't have the money."

"That's what stumped me for a while. I could see the robbery angle but not what it did for RMD, LLC. I did some creative thinking. What would RMD, LLC get out of this? I got the answer very late in the game. The FinCEN agents took legal paper possession of the cash in the vault, so when it went missing, the feds had to cover the loss. That was no problem for the feds because ten million dollars is not even chicken feed in their world. They controlled the money, and it was gone. So the feds had to compensate RMD, LLC for the loss. They could not admit the money was gone, so the agents did an end-around-run. The legal beagles in their department got North Carolina Mutual Indemnity to cover the loss, and the feds would quietly compensate North Carolina Mutual Indemnity for the ten million dollars. Suddenly the problem went away. No money was stolen. No insurance fraud was suspected. The Swensen Armored Car Company was not on the hook for any loss."

"So what's the problem?"

"I was thinking the same until yesterday. Doing my due diligence, I asked to see the paperwork from North Carolina Mutual Indemnity for the loss. The paperwork was very interesting. The check was drafted on a North Carolina Mutual Indemnity financial certificate, but the recipient was the First Sandersonville Bank of Trust. In essence and on paper, the money from RMD, LLC jumped over RMD, LLC's head. He went directly from North Carolina Mutual Indemnity to the First Sandersonville Bank of Trust."

"So?"

"RMD, LLC money was marijuana money. Since marijuana is a Schedule One drug, banks cannot handle marijuana money. So RMD, LLC was in the difficult position of having ten million dollars in legal money that it could not put in a bank. But, and this was a big *but*, if the known marijuana money could be converted into a legal financial instrument, banks could handle the money."

"So?"

"So everything this past week has been to convert legal marijuana money into legal federal money, into a legal financial instrument a bank can legally handle. *Legally.* That's what the entire dematerializing armored truck matter has been about. It has been a cover to convert ten million dollars legal marijuana money into a ten-million-dollar check that could be legally invested. Everyone got a piece of the pie. Steigle and the Jacksons walked away with ten million dollars. Charlie got the Swensen mechanical shop, and Harry Sandusky got his loss covered. Your nephew and Ramon had nothing to do with the scam, but they are going to end up with the Swensen business."

"What about me? What do I get out of it?"

"Now that is a good question. I wondered about that because I view you as an honorable man. I don't know, but I can guess. Your nephew said you had cancer, but it's in remission. That might be what you told him, and it might not be true. If you are not in remission, stated bluntly, you are on your way out, and there is no need for you to scramble for dollars. Or you are in remission, but don't trust the doctor's prognosis. Either way, you want out of the business. You're older than me, and, like me, you know you don't have many more years left. Money is not a motivator in your life. You've got enough money. Even more important, there are people like me who figure things out. The last thing you want is to spend one second behind bars for stealing a few dollars. As long as you did not end up with money, you cannot be charged with anything."

"And no crime has been committed."

"No crime has been committed." Noonan pointed at the logbooks in the box by the door. "So I'm returning your logbooks and wishing you the best of whatever time you—and I—have left."

Swensen just smiled as Noonan rose to leave the office. Noonan stalled for a moment and then turned back to Swensen. "Funny thing," Noonan said with a false look of puzzlement on his face. "When I came here last Monday, one of the things you told me was the drivers of the armored truck that was never missing had communicated with the garage that they were being foamed."

"And?"

"That conversation never made it into the logbooks," Noonan said, pointing at the cardboard box of logbooks next to the door. "Neither Ramon nor your nephew knew anything about foam, so the call could not have come in over the Swensen Armored Car Company regular communication system. Those two are quite competent. If the call had been logged in, they would have found it. But when I asked them about foam, they didn't know what I was talking about."

"I guess the call came in on my private cell phone."

"I thought that might be the case," Noonan said. "Probably a short call. Hmm, yes, a short call. Very short. Just short enough if any law-enforcement organization asked for everyone's cell phone and traced numbers for that day, *someone* would have a very good answer as to why he—or she—received a short phone call just about the time the armored truck vanished into the ether."

"It's a wonderful theory," Swensen said, smiling. "But no law-enforcement organization has asked for any cell-phone records because no crime has been committed."

"True. I have one last item. There is a security camera in the vault. I saw it when I counted the RMD, LLC money. FinCEN told me yesterday's tape was missing."

"Odd. I had not heard that."

"Interesting. You see, that tape would have recorded all the activity in the vault from the time the missing armored truck showed up until the moment Steigle left on his run. That would reasonably have been the time when the RMD, LLC money disappeared."

"I thought the RMD, LLC moneys had been seized by FinCEN."

"So they say. But the security tape for the time period is missing. Gone. Steigle could not have taken it because he was on the road. The Sandersonville Police do not have it because the security tape they are examining is from the garage. To see if we can figure out how the dematerializing armored car reappeared."

"How unusual. What do you think happened to the tape from the vault?"

"Gremlins. I think the gremlins took it. It's not in the recording machine or the vault. FinCEN does not have it, and the Sandersonville Police do not have it. The vault personnel have been in lockdown, so they do not have it. Steigle was on the road when it went missing. None of the police or FinCEN people have access to the vault. You, of course, were whisking around the garage and offices responding to questions." Noonan continued. "I guess a Gremlin took it. But, actually, and in reality, the tape is not needed. No crime has been committed. The RMD, LLC moneys were legally seized by FinCEN and transported by the agency to a location unknown to me. Or you. North Carolina Mutual Indemnity is going to cover the seizure with a check to RMD, LLC. The dematerializing armored truck—I like that adjective—has been returned. The Jacksons are in the Bahamas and not about to return any time soon. The only missing piece of this puzzle—if it is a puzzle at all—is Steigle, and there is not a shred of evidence he committed any crime. He's just missing. When he returns, he may talk with you. But then, again, he's a lawyer. And a very good one."

"What you have said is true. A Gremlin must have taken the tape. But since no crime has been committed, there is no reason for the security tape to be considered as evidence."

"It would only be evidence if a crime had been committed. Which, everyone says, has not happened."

"True, true," Noonan said. "But a word to wise. There's an old adage in the law-enforcement business I recall. It goes something like this: 'Robberies are like peanuts; you can't stop at just one.'"

"How quaint. I'll keep it in mind in my retirement."

"A good attitude. I'd hate to see you again under similar circumstances." And with that last comment, Noonan was gone.

Chapter 41

Joseph Richiamo was neither displeased nor annoyed when he arrived at the Sandersonville Coffee Shoppe for a mug with Noonan. Richiamo had a vacation tan—in his case, ruddy.

"I've never been here," Richiamo said as he took his skinny vanilla latte and sat down. "Has it been here long?"

"I'm not a coffee drinker," Noonan admitted. "So I don't know. I just wanted to have a chat with you in an out-of-the-way place."

"Well, you chose well. What can I do for you? As far as I know, everything is settled."

"True, true. As far as the law is concerned, everything is settled."

"And the insurance company. We were very happy with our check."

"But you didn't get a check. First Sandersonville Bank of Trust got the check."

"That is correct. You are diligent in your homework, I must say."

"Do you mind if I ask what the check paid for?"

"Well, you know, it's a matter of confidentiality. I represent a number of clients who have made investments, and they don't want their names bandied about."

"Especially if the money is marijuana money."

"Not true. Not a dime of the check that went to First Sandersonville Bank of Trust was marijuana money. It was a North Carolina Mutual Indemnity check guaranteed by the United States government."

"True. And very clever, I must say."

"I," Richiamo gave a look of perfect innocence, "do not know what you are talking about. Everything has been done is legal and above board."

"Oh, I agree with you," Noonan said, and Richiamo relaxed.

A bit.

"Why are we having this conversation?"

"Personal interest," Noonan said. "There's no question what has transpired is legal. But there is a lingering question. All the activity—"

"Legal activity," Richiamo cut in.

"True," responded Noonan. "All the activity, legal activity, has taken place here in Sandersonville. Yet you, and presumably the legal marijuana money, are from out of Colorado."

"So? The money is legal in Colorado, and it is legal to cross state lines with legal money. That's right out of the United States Constitution."

"True. But I'm not maneuvering down that road. I punched up RMD, LLC on the State of Colorado web page and discovered it has only been in business for two years."

"True. I have only been in business for two years."

"It's also the first time the name Richiamo pops up on the web."

"Well, I guess you could say I'm two people. I'm the *R* in RMD, LLC—legally, let me add. And I changed my name recently to become Joseph Richiamo."

"Do you speak Italian?"

"No. Where did that come from?"

"Out of thin air. You don't have to answer, but I'm betting you had legal help with the name change and setting up the corporation in Colorado."

"Well, yes. You can't be too careful these days."

"I agree with you there. Did you happen to get legal help from a law firm by the name of Inganno?"

Now Richiamo was antsy with suspicion.

"Why?"

"No particular reason. And nothing to worry about because nothing illegal has happened."

"You got that right." He was emphatic.

"I just find it interesting someone from Colorado would have connections in a little town on the North Carolina coast."

"Well, these things do happen."

"Uh-huh. What was your name before it was Richiamo?"

"George."

"George what?"

"Sandusky."

"Any relation to Harry Sandusky of North Carolina Mutual Indemnity?"

"He's my brother."